COCKY PLAYBOY

ALEX WOLF

SLOANE HOWELL

He's a bastard in Burberry.

Decker Collins knows how to do one thing—win.

When his billion-dollar law practice moves to merge with a firm out of Dallas, *she* shows up to oversee the transition.

Tate Reynolds—the vixen in Versace.

She's whip-smart, sassy, and gorgeous. Oh, and she doesn't take any of Decker's sh*t.

With the merger hanging in the balance, they go to war with each other.

There's only one problem. This war isn't just about business.

Because when they're not butting heads…

They're banging headboards.

Publisher © Alex Wolf & Sloane Howell October 4th, 2019
Cover Design: Alex Wolf
Editor: Underline This Editing
Formatting: Alex Wolf

TATE

NOTHING in my life can ever be easy.

I glance at the clock on the wall of my hotel suite. I knew this would happen. Weston knows I hate getting assignments at the last minute and rushing to prepare. I'm going to be late. I'm *never* late. He's probably already on his first drink at the bar. I could use a drink about now.

I make it a priority to be organized and professional. It's impossible when he throws stuff at me and makes unreasonable demands. My temples throb with the tension headache slowly radiating through my brain. I rub my fingers in soothing circles above my eyes, hoping to escape the pain. In haste, I toss a few Advil in my mouth, take a drink of water, and toss my head back to swallow.

The room is nicer than I imagined for a quick trip: queen-sized bed, high thread-count sheets, walk in shower, hardwood floors. I shouldn't expect any less from Weston. He's a heavy hitter.

I need to get my ass in gear and out of this hotel room. Weston Hunter is not the kind of man you keep waiting. He runs one of the most successful law firms in Dallas—The Hunter Group. He brought me to Chicago to aid in a merger that could be huge for our firm. It's an amazing, though stressful, opportunity. I can't help but feel this is my big test. Trial by fire.

I'm a senior associate and this is my shot at making partner.

I'm the best lawyer at the firm. It's not a brag, Weston's told me before.

However, I'm underprepared and that doesn't sit well with me. Back in the Dallas office I was reading over a deposition when Weston barged in and hollered for me to grab a bag and meet him at the airport. I don't know what he was thinking.

Maybe he's the boss and can do as he pleases?

I fuss over my hair one last time in the mirror. There's one strand that refuses to behave. This shit happens when I'm in a hurry. Everything falls apart.

Giving up on my hair, I slip on a pair of black heels and smooth my hand down the front of my skirt. I pick a stray piece of lint from the back as I twist around in the mirror. My blouse appears crisp and wrinkle free. My jacket completes the ensemble.

Finally, all the paperwork is organized into neat piles on the coffee table. Lists of clients, checklists of shit that needs done for due diligence. It's all there. I breathe easy, gather the files, and tuck the hotel key into my wristlet.

Satisfied I have everything, I walk from the room and get on the elevator. It moves at a snail's pace. If I wasn't afraid of working up a sweat, I'd have taken the stairs to get me to the lobby faster. It never fails; the minute I'm in a hurry, Father Time makes things stand still. It'd be just my luck for the thing to stop working.

I watch the numbers slowly change from one floor to the next. To make things better, I'm stuck with an older woman wearing enough perfume to choke a horse. I hope the freesia scent doesn't cling to my clothes.

Arriving in the lobby, I barely give the concierge time to open the door as I rush out to the street in hopes of catching a cab. I wave my hand at one passing by, calling out, "Taxi!" and it rolls to a stop.

Perfect timing for once.

I make it four steps when a shoulder slams into me out of nowhere. My folder flies through the air. The papers explode like a flock of pigeons and float down to the sidewalk. Catching my balance after managing not to snap a heel, I watch in horror as my hard work scatters itself along the sidewalk.

I throw my hands up. "Really?"

What are the chances?

I shake my head. It'll be a miracle if the wind doesn't carry my papers off to the suburbs of Chicago. I let out an annoyed huff and glance to the perpetrator who caused this misfortune. My eyes start at his Berluti shoes and work their way up a Burberry three-piece that's tailored perfectly to his frame. Icy blue eyes meet my gaze paired with a mischievous smirk. A smirk that would no doubt be sexy under different circumstances. Damn, he's hot. His smoldering stare is something out of the movies.

"You could have said excuse me, or sorry at least." I narrow my eyes on him then drop down to gather my papers. His cologne lands in my nose and smells so good it should be banned. Warmth spreads through my veins as I inhale the intoxicating scent.

A low snicker passes between his perfectly sculpted lips. "You bumped into me, *sweetheart*." His voice is low and comes out like a primal growl that would make me weak in the knees if he wasn't such an arrogant prick.

I suck in a breath and get a grip on myself, shaking off the sexual thoughts rushing to the forefront of my mind. It's just that I have a thing for sexy voices. Sure, I love a good-looking man as much as the next single woman, but give me a deep voice that vibrates down to my core and it does something to me. This jerk has the voice and the looks that go with it. I bet that neatly trimmed beard would work wonders against my thighs.

Regardless of my impure thoughts, he picked the wrong woman to mess with.

"Sweetheart?" I roll my eyes. "No. I recall the moment perfectly. You barreled into me and nearly knocked me to the ground." I glance to the sidewalk. "Look at my papers."

I watch his eyes flit from my cleavage to the strewn papers on the ground and back to my breasts. He makes no attempt to hide the fact he's ogling the twins.

I point two fingers at him then at my face as I speak. "My eyes are right here, buddy."

He stares like I'm on a display, put there solely for his amusement. Those blue eyes cut into me like glaciers. "Buddy." He snorts. "Have to admit, I like the view of you on your knees in front of me."

"In your dreams, pal."

"Highly doubtful." He rubs his jaw, still smirking. Those blue eyes pierce straight through me once more.

He must see I'm thinking about what he said, me on my knees in front of him. I bet he's hung like a damn horse. Jerks usually are, in my experience anyway. I mentally smack myself. I need to snap out of it.

Sneering, I move to gather my papers.

The hottie in the suit bends down to help. He reaches for my folder, and I smack his large hand.

"I've got it." Cute or not, this guy is an ass and gets on my last nerve. Not to mention nobody touches my work. Nobody!

"Have a nice evening." He huffs out a breath and has the nerve to climb into my cab.

"What the hell?" I yell at him and throw my hand up. "That's *my* cab. I'm in a hurry."

He shoots me a sly wink. A grin spreads across his

smug face and his pearly whites flash. "I'm in a hurry too, *sweetheart*." He smacks the door of the cab twice. "Spoils of war."

"Asshole!"

The cab speeds off.

I grind my teeth and continue trying to make heads or tails of the mess he's left me in. This is just great. Now, I have to go back into the hotel and fix everything. All my hard work is ruined. The papers are all out of order. Hours of my life wasted.

My phone pings, and I know it's Weston ready to chew my ass out for not being there. It's not like I'm wasting his time on purpose. Rain drops plop on my head and thrum on the ground, and at this moment, I don't know how things could get any worse. I clutch everything under my arm and run as fast as my heels allow back into the hotel lobby before the rain ruins my hair.

Shaking my head, I hop back in the elevator and make it to my room. One glance in the mirror and rage consumes me. I look like a wet rat with smudged makeup. Grabbing a towel, I wrap my hair up and hustle to get organized once more. If I ever see that bastard again, he's a dead man.

WALKING into the bar thirty minutes late, I'm surprised to find Weston still there. I square my shoulders and approach. He's perched on a stool nursing a tumbler of whiskey. I lay the files on the stained oak bar top and situate myself on the stool next to him.

He rubs his chin. His eyes are two dark slits and burn a hole into me. I know I messed up, but it wasn't my fault.

"Where the hell have you been?" His voice is low but lethal. "Why didn't you answer the phone?" He grips the glass and taps the side for the bartender to pour him a refill.

"You done?"

Weston doesn't respond. He simply takes a long swig of the dark brown liquid.

"I would've been here half an hour ago if some jerk didn't knock my papers everywhere and steal my cab. Then came the damn rain." I huff out a breath and that stupid curl springs to my forehead. I blow it out of my eyes and wait for Weston to respond. I'm sure he's going to rip my ass and threaten to fire me, but with the mood I'm in, I almost welcome it so I can argue with him. We both know he won't follow through on any threats and I need to let off some steam.

Weston halfway laughs to himself.

"What?" I shoot a glare in his direction.

"Nothing, that's just how I met Brooke. Stole her cab. Granted I didn't knock her on her ass."

I narrow my eyes and try to reclaim some amount of dignity. Through gritted teeth I say, "He *didn't* knock me on my ass."

Weston sighs. "Whatever, Decker left already. Got tired of waiting. You made me look incompetent."

"I'm not a miracle worker. I warned you I didn't have enough time to get everything ready. I'd barely checked in when you demanded this shit." I pat the folder I carried in. "Did you want half-assed work? Because that's *not* what you pay me for, and you know it."

"Whatever. You win." He shakes his head and orders me a drink. "You look like you need one. Just make sure you're prepared for the meeting tomorrow."

I smirk. "I always am, when given an *appropriate* amount of time." I knock back the drink. I deserve it after the day I've had. Weston settles the bill.

"Tate?"

"Yeah?"

He grins and nods at my head. "Do something about that hair."

I scowl back at him. *Asshole.*

He snickers.

I know it looks like a ball of fuzz on my head after the rain and towel drying it. It couldn't be helped.

Weston stands up. "Let's head back to the hotel. You can get room service and fix whatever this shit's supposed to be." He motions to the papers hanging from my file.

I had them all color-coded at least. I suppose they could be worse.

We share a cab back and go our separate ways in the

lobby. Arriving in my room, I toss the files on the table and kick off my heels. I trade my business attire for my robe. Falling into the couch, I grab the menu for room service and scan the choices available. With a big day tomorrow, I don't want anything heavy. I settle on a grilled chicken salad and a fruit bowl for dessert. The files can wait until after I eat. What I really want is a nice warm soak in the tub. That stupid jerk and his mesmerizing blue eyes. My cheeks flush and heat spreads down my neck and across my chest at the thought of his face between my legs.

On my knees my ass, buddy. Put your mouth where it belongs.

My mind flashes to his smoldering stare. It's been too long since I've had sex. That's all these thoughts are. But I can't get him out of my head. His stupid smirk. His deep voice. His large hands. That heavenly cologne. It's like I can still smell it. And for God's sake, that cocky wink he threw my way as he took off in my cab.

The saddest part is, it's his arrogance that's doing things to me. I don't want him to be sweet. I want him to be commanding and dominate me, but I want him to work for it. I want to put up a fight and make him earn every inch.

My fingers trail between my breasts as the fantasy plays out in my mind. I pinch one of my nipples and picture those striking blue eyes. He was gorgeous. I want him to make some smartass comment so I can shove my pussy on his mouth to shut him up. I smirk at the thought as my fingers move farther south. I picture that devilish grin as the tip of my finger circles my clit.

A rap at the door echoes through the room, interrupting my fantasy.

I jump. *Shit.*

"Room service."

"Coming!" I shake my head at my choice of word and attempt to stifle the laugh building in my chest. I yank my robe closed and head for the door. I don't have on a bra and don't want the guy thinking his tip is me flashing my breasts. I open the door and a younger man wheels a cart in. I tell him thanks and grab some cash from my wallet to give him a decent gratuity because I feel guilty about what I was doing, even though he has no clue. He gives me a polite thank you and is on his way.

I walk to the bathroom and wet my face with a cool cloth and get ready to eat and forget about those blue eyes and that smart mouth.

I smother my salad in Italian dressing and stab a chunk of chicken with my fork. My stomach growls as I chew. I hadn't realized how hungry I was until now.

Despite the food, I can't stop thinking about that guy. I'm here for a job not to meet Mr. Wrong. That's all that cocky man would be. Another jerk to cross off the list of men who can't handle me.

I know I'm difficult to please. Working in a male dominated field I have to be. I can dish it out with the best of them. Some men appreciate I can hold my own while others find it intimidating. Putting up walls helps keep things professional and focused on work abilities, not how I look in a skirt.

Tomorrow should be interesting. We're meeting with a group of brothers who run a huge law firm here. The Hunter Group is merging with them. I can't help but wonder if they're anything like Weston and the guys back in Dallas.

DECKER

I HOPE today's meeting with Weston and his senior associate goes better than yesterday's attempt. I stopped by the bar, Label Fifty-one, but had to skip out early to meet up with my current fuck buddy. At least I got the letter of intent signed while Weston was there. No backing out of the merger now.

Anyway, the fuck buddy… she works in pediatrics. She's a surgeon and just as busy as me, if not more so. She knows the deal and doesn't expect our relationship to go anywhere outside of the hotel suites we meet up in. She's career driven, and I respect that about her. I admire a woman who knows what she wants and goes for it. Yesterday was our last fling and it was perfect. There were no emotions tied to it at all. We both knew the score, and it was simply about physical release.

The position she's been vying for in LA landed in her lap last week. She leaves today, actually. I sent her some flowers wishing her the best. I know I'll never hear from her again and I don't expect to. I'm good with that. It is what it is.

The sex was good but neither of us recognized it as anything more than a basic need. I'm a busy man with a lot on my plate. Getting emotionally involved with someone is the last thing I need.

Weston and I were supposed to go over some high-level plans for the merger, but his associate never showed up. I desperately need this union with The Hunter Group to be a success. Maybe, after it's complete, I could think about meeting someone long-term. I'd have more time. Right now, it's just not possible.

I've known Weston Hunter since my college days, but that doesn't mean I can afford to not take this seriously. In my private bathroom, I straighten my tie once more. I want Weston to be on board with everything that needs to happen. I have to make sure my people are taken care of in the long-term as well as the short-term. If we can pull it off, there is a lot of mutual benefit to go around the table.

I exit the bathroom and make my way through the office while giving everything a once over. Quinn, my assistant, has assured me everything is in place, but I'm not risking it. There's no room for mistakes. Everything has to be perfect. It's tough to be taken seriously, given my past. Most people see my name and it conjures up images of what they've read in tabloids or seen on gossip sites. None of it has anything to do with what I can do in a courtroom.

I pass my two younger brothers, the twins, Deacon and Dexter. Dexter has a scar over his left brow from a skateboard accident, and tattoos barely peek out from under his suit. It's the only way most people can tell them apart. Dexter scared the shit out of the whole family when he crashed on a makeshift ramp in our driveway. There was so much blood I thought he was dead. I just knew Mom was going to kill me because I was supposed to be watching him and he was trying to show off in front of my friends.

Deacon walks ahead repositioning a few pens, then puts them back where they were. He looks up to verify I'm watching as he grins.

I silently curse him under my breath. They both love fucking with me, have since we were kids.

Dexter laughs.

Deacon glances at me and holds his hands up in mock surrender. "Just making sure they're perfectly aligned with a proper radius to maximize client reach potential. Can't have anyone leaning over too far and have their tie land in a cup of coffee."

Dexter holds in a laugh and looks like he might piss himself.

Deacon maintains a perfect deadpan stare and turns to Quinn. "Might want to check the chairs with a tape measure. Make sure they're all four inches from the edge of the table. Four inches, Quinn. Not five, not three. Four! I saw a few that might be outside a tolerable variance. Don't forget to wipe them down with sanitizer."

Dexter has to turn and stare at the wall to try and compose himself.

I clench my jaw and do my best to ignore them. They love to talk shit and get me riled up. Any other day I would give in and laugh with them. I can be self-deprecating when I need to be. But today is different. I know they don't get how important this is to me. They can afford to goof off. They may be partners, but they don't actively manage the firm, and this deal isn't riding on their asses. The deal I haven't told them about yet, because I don't want to hear their shit. I'll deal with that later.

"Quinn, is the coffee fresh?"

Quinn glares at Deacon, and when I turn around to face her, she schools her features in a hurry. "Yes, Mr. Collins. Everything is ready to go."

Deacon grins at her. "Did you check the temperature? Needs to be a sweltering one hundred…"

I've finally had enough and shoot him a glare that says *shut the fuck up, now.*

He silences immediately.

I turn back to Quinn. "You're sure it's fresh?"

I can tell she's slightly annoyed, given that she pays as much attention to detail as I do, but like a good employee she puts on a smile and reassures me for the thousandth time.

I turn around to get one last look. Everything really does look great. The long table has a file sitting in front of each chair with our company branding on the front. The coffee, water, croissants, donuts, and juice are neatly on display on a table at the back of the room. Quinn will be on hand to serve everyone and to assist me if I need her.

Donavan, my third brother, walks into the conference room and stands stiff as a board like a soldier in front of me. "Sorry I'm late, *Drill Sergeant*!" He hollers the last two words and drags out the syllables like we're on the set of *Full Metal Jacket*.

They all die laughing.

I lower my voice and try not to grin. "You motherfuckers about finished?" I shoot all three of them a dirty look then straighten Donavan's tie. I'm not even going to ask why it's so damn crooked. I already have a good idea what he's been up to this morning, judging by the lipstick stain on the collar of his shirt. I'd hate to see his dry-cleaning bill with the way he goes through women and suits.

Deacon walks up, finally serious. "Lighten up, bro. You're going to stroke out if you don't keep your blood pressure down."

"Needs to stroke something," says Donavan. "Relieve some pressure." He waggles his eyebrows at me.

I grip the Windsor knot on his tie and shove it up

toward his neck a little harder than I need to, as if I'm straightening it.

He starts to choke, and finally it's me who gets to laugh.

Children. That's exactly what they are.

If I wasn't afraid of Weston being on his way in right now, I'd throttle all of them. "We're done joking. They'll be here soon." I take a step back and wave a finger in front of all three of their faces. "You assholes fuck up this meeting and you'll be proofreading trusts in the goddamn…"

I hear a throat clear and turn to see Quinn is at the doorway. Weston is behind her, and there's a woman with him, but I can't see her yet, just a pair of tanned calves and heels. "Mr. Hunter and Ms. Reynolds for you, sir."

"Thanks, Quinn."

She nods and turns to them.

I glare at my brothers who scurry like fleas to take their seats. They're lucky I love them. I'm doing this as much for them as I am for me. I'm not the only one who will benefit, though I'd be lying if I didn't say some days I dream of what it would've been like if I were an only child. A hell of a lot less stressful, that's for damn sure. I do love them, though. They're assholes, but I wouldn't trade them for anything.

Weston Hunter, head of The Hunter Group, fills the doorway. He's a bit of a prick, just like me, and he knows it. It's probably why we get along so well. I don't know how Brooke, his wife, puts up with him. He shoots me a smug grin as we shake hands, and Quinn shows him to his seat. As he strolls through the room greeting and shaking hands with my brothers, I look behind him.

No. Fucking. Way.

My breath catches in my throat. It's the damn woman I ran into on the sidewalk yesterday in front of the hotel. The smoking-hot one. If I'm being totally honest, I pictured her while I was banging Jessica for the last time. There was just something about her. She was so damn sassy and defiant—flustered. And now, she's walking right into my conference room.

I watch and wait for her to recognize me. It would be highly entertaining if I didn't have so much at stake with this deal.

She's ridiculously sexy. I'll give her that. Her tan legs are lethal in the form-fitting skirt she's wearing. Her spiked, pointy-toed heels would feel good digging into my ass. I can picture her legs wrapped around me as I thrust into her.

What the fuck are you doing? Compose yourself.

Her dirty-blonde hair is pinned neatly to her head other than the one curl she keeps fidgeting with behind her ear. I want to kiss her there, right in that spot, and watch her blush. Like she did yesterday in the street.

Those lovely honey-brown eyes meet mine.

It takes all of a split-second for the recognition to set

in. At first, it's surprise, then she scowls at me like she could tear my head off and shit down my throat.

Without thinking, I smirk at her and shoot her a wink. Fuck, I hope my brothers didn't notice or Weston for that matter. I can't seem to help myself. There's something about her. Something that gets under my skin in the best and worst ways possible.

"Decker Collins." I shoot her my best crowd pleaser smile.

"Tate Reynolds." Her words are short and laced with venom.

My cock twitches at the sound of her voice and scent of her perfume. Cinnamon and vanilla? Smells like a damn cinnamon roll I'd love to sink my teeth into. She looks poised—all business. I bet I could break right through her tough demeanor, though. Grip her by the hair and smack her ass once, and she'd be all mine. Despite my best attempts, my mind races with dirty thoughts of sending everyone out of the damn room and bending her over the table to find out.

I'd lift her skirt and rip her panties. Bite her neck and pull her hair just to hear her moan. She'd pretend to fight it at first, with her sassy attitude, trying to have the upper hand, but before I was done, she'd be begging for more.

I look down and realize I'm still shaking her hand as she tries to pull away.

What the hell is wrong with me?

TATE

I TAKE my seat feeling those blue eyes I dreamed of last night lighting a fire in my chest. It makes me hate him all over again, that he can have this effect on me. I'm Tate Reynolds. I can hold my own with any man in a suit. I shouldn't be letting this prick toy with my emotions. I damn sure shouldn't be attracted to him.

"Missed you yesterday for drinks, Tate." The jerk from yesterday stares at me, clearly amused with himself. His lips are curved upward, his eyes meet mine, and I swear the man is laughing on the inside at this cruel twist of fate the universe has played on us. I remember it all too well. How good he smelled. How attractive he was and still is. The man is perfection in the looks and voice department. Too bad the asshole seems to be in charge of things here. The universe is a real dick sometimes.

"It's Ms. Reynolds." Tate is my name but that's too personal, and this is work.

Weston leans in as Decker Collins—of course he has a hot name—gets on with his PowerPoint presentation outlining the overview of the merger.

As my eyes dart around the table, his associates appear confused.

Weston whisper-growls in my ear, "What the fuck is your problem with Decker?" I know he isn't pleased with my behavior and he can read body-language like a hawk. Couple that with the way I spoke to Decker and Weston looks like he'd pounce on me if we weren't in the middle of a meeting.

The bastard had the nerve to wink at me when no one was paying attention. If he wants my approval, he's going about it the wrong way. I'm not some little tart he can shoot a flirtatious smile at to get his way. I'm Texas born and bred. I'm as tough if not tougher than any man in this room. I can hold my own.

I whisper, "He was the guy who stole my cab and made me late."

Weston snickers and shakes his head. "Of course he was." His eyes narrow. "It's done now. Whatever happened yesterday doesn't exist. You need to be professional."

I feel like a child who's had her hand smacked for sticking it in the candy drawer in the kitchen. And I'll be damned if Decker Collins isn't a piece of candy I'd like to sample. He's infuriating. He makes a

PowerPoint presentation sexy. How is that even possible?

I try not to sulk in my seat as Weston takes over talking about the merger between our two firms and how they'll be absorbed into The Hunter Group and the appropriate steps moving forward.

Decker's brothers look around the room like they want to jump out the window. Something is off.

"What is all this?" I think the guy's name is Donavan, and he's damn near seething as he stares at Decker. They all look like cardboard cutouts of one another, but Donavan has slightly different features than the others. Deacon and Dexter appear to be identical twins except one of them has a scar over his eye. I have no idea how their mother kept track of all of them with their looks and names. It's quite a chore.

"What merger?" says Deacon.

"You're selling the firm?" says Dexter.

I look to Weston during the outburst and interruption, but he's staring at Decker Collins with a *what the fuck* expression on his face. He's not exactly angry, but he isn't happy. Looks like Decker Collins didn't tell his brothers about his plans for the firm.

Decker pushes his chair back, stands up, and puts both his palms on the table, commanding the room as he towers over the rest of us with a look of pure power and dominance. Man can he rock a suit like nobody's business. I hadn't realized how tall the smug jerk was until now. With a stern expression on his face, he glares at his brothers and says, "This merger is in the best interest of everyone in this room. A letter of intent has been signed. It's happening. Get on board."

The men continue arguing as though Weston and I aren't here. I know when to fight my battles and right now isn't the time. It is kind of shitty that he didn't discuss it with anyone. He's the only managing partner, but still. The man is a definite egomaniac.

Weston remains composed and nods toward the table at the back of the room. That's my cue to make an escape. I'm here to back up Weston, not assert my opinion on family matters.

I slip off to the back where Decker's assistant stands by the table with the food spread. The whole meeting is a disaster, but I can tell Weston isn't thrown off by the family drama. He looks amused, like this isn't his first rodeo with the Collins boys. The man is used to family squabbles anyway, so he'll be able to smooth this over far better than I could. He has a firm with his own brothers, so I guess it's relatable for him. Things have gotten heated between them in the past as well. Everyone wants to be the leader of the pack. The room is full of alpha males who all think they're the boss. I feel dizzy with the testosterone cocktail that's filled the air.

I accept the assistant's offer for a cup of coffee and ignore the brooding suits until Weston finally interjects and puts a stop to all the bickering.

"Listen, Decker. I don't know what's going on

here, but I trust you'll get your house in order. I have a flight back to Dallas I can't miss." Weston pushes up his sleeve and glances at his watch. I can see annoyance flickering in his eyes. He's always on a tight schedule trying to balance the business and his family life.

I have none of that on my plate. My career comes first always. I can't remember the last time I had a steady boyfriend. Most men are intimidated by me because I can beat them in the courtroom and best them at their own sports.

"Tate will be staying on a day-to-day basis to transition everything smoothly. She'll be doing due diligence, checking for conflicts of interest, making introductions to clients. She's more than capable of handling whatever you need."

I nearly spit out my coffee. Did he just say he was leaving me here until the merger is complete? No way. He must be insane. Did he not listen to a thing I told him earlier about his friend? Not to mention, I'm not prepared.

Decker smirks at me and shoots me another stupid wink. I scowl at him and Weston. What's Weston thinking? I can't work side by side with this asshole. I move toward Weston once the meeting is over and the room has cleared. "What did you mean you're leaving me here to see things through? I can do this from Dallas."

"I meant exactly what I said. I need you here. You'll

need to meet with clients and I want you close to this, keeping an eye on shit."

"I just… I don't know if I can work with him."

"I thought I told you yesterday didn't happen."

"Come on. You weren't there. You didn't hear how he spoke to me. The guy is a major jackass."

Weston shakes his head, clearly still pissed off about the way the meeting went, and now he's having to deal with me.

I already know I shouldn't have said anything. I should keep my head down and do my damn job, but Christ, I really don't know if I can work with Decker Collins without murdering the winking son of a bitch. I can already tell his brothers hate my guts.

Weston puts hands on both my shoulders and makes sure the Collins brothers aren't paying attention. "I can't believe I have to say this to you of all people, Tate. But I don't give a flying fuck what happened about a cab. You're an adult. Grow up and do your damn job."

I swallow my pride. I'm being a brat. I know I am. I don't know why Decker gets to me, but he does. That man makes me want to choke him… or kiss him. I put on my best all-business face and nod. "No, you're right. I apologize. Consider it done."

"Good. I don't want to hear anything else about it. Decker is a good guy, you'll see. I've known him for years. I know you can handle him. This is an opportunity to level up, Tate. You've never let me down before. Don't start now."

My chest swells with pride. This is my shot.

I nod and he returns it. I walk him out as we go over the finer details about my living arrangement for the duration of my stay. I'm given a company card for allowances, meals, and professional attire. Not that I'm concerned with money, but it's a nice perk of the job. I bring in a lot of big clients to the firm and Weston rewards me handsomely for it. We part ways and I stop and wait for an elevator.

I watch as Weston walks into Decker's office and hope I can pull off the impossible. When I turn around, the Collins brothers stand in the hallway staring at me. They definitely do not look happy I'll be sticking around. For some reason, I can't stand there and look at their ridiculous stares. I walk off and go in search of the bathroom to get my shit together. I'm a professional. There's no way they'll get to me. I just need to go scream into the toilet or flush myself down it first.

Damn Decker Collins and those blue eyes.

DECKER

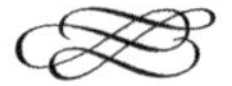

"WELL THAT COULD HAVE GONE OVER BETTER. What the fuck did you ambush them for?"

I ignore Weston's question. I have my reasons. "They'll come around," I tell Weston as he helps himself to a drink from the shelf behind my desk. "So will your associate." I grin and take the drink he poured for me. "You know I bumped into her yesterday… on the sidewalk outside of her hotel."

"And?"

"She's easy on the eyes and has… personality." I take another sip of whiskey and think about how sexy she looks when she gets all flustered and angry. I bet she's insane in bed. Bet she'd scratch her nails down my back. I'd love to have her saying my name as I fucked an orgasm out of her.

Weston gives me a look like he can read my thoughts. The dirty ones I'm having about Tate

Reynolds and ripping her tight skirt down her legs and spanking her ass over my desk for being a smartass during the meeting.

"She may have mentioned you were the one who ruined her day, but I am warning you now, Tate is a professional and she'll chew your goddamn head off and spit it out. I'm not bullshitting. She is a fucking shark."

"I have enough shit to worry about without fucking someone in my office. You know me better than that. And you of all people understand the ramifications. I know what's at stake." I don't shit where I eat. Nothing will happen with the woman, despite my impure thoughts. I can't say I was never tempted in the past, but I keep work and my personal life completely separate. Tate is very tempting, but I won't let anything get in the way of this deal.

"Indeed." Weston raises his rocks glass.

Quinn buzzes me. "The car is downstairs to take Mr. Hunter to the airport, sir."

"That's my cue to leave you to the wolves." Weston shakes my hand and leaves me to deal with my asshole brothers. The door closes and I fall back on the leather sofa in the corner of my office that overlooks Millennium Park. If I want to see Lake Michigan, I can see it from the roof deck. I go there often to clear my head. It's my favorite spot.

I know I have about two minutes before my asshat brothers barge in demanding answers. It'll be even worse now that Weston's gone. Rubbing my temples, I pop an aspirin and prepare to defend my choice in merging the firm. I've worked my goddamn ass off to build this place up, but The Hunter Group will take us to the next level.

I buzz Quinn.

"Yes, Mr. Collins?"

"Put Tate in the corner office. The one with the gorgeous view of the lake."

That office is at the other end of the floor. I'm putting her there because having some distance between us will make it easier. I'm physically attracted to the woman and need to keep things strictly professional between us no matter how hard my cock grows at her smartass remarks.

"Give her a tour and anything else she needs."

"Yes, sir."

"Thank you."

"You're most welcome."

My office door bursts open, and my brothers quickly fill the room.

"Don't you assholes know how to knock?" I take another sip of whiskey. I'm going to need it to put up with them. The three of them enter the room and take up the three hardback leather chairs facing my desk.

"I thought you were building the firm up for the family? This was supposed to be our legacy and what, you're just gonna sell us out to the Hunter Group?"

"What part of merger don't you get? Every single

thing I'm doing is for the good of this firm and all of you. Nothing has changed. It's going to be better for everyone. You'll see. Being under The Hunter umbrella will bring us more clients which means more billable hours. We can hire more attorneys and take a lot of the workload off ourselves. Our current growth rate can't sustain what we're doing. We'll meet our goals faster with less of the work. I don't get why you're so upset." I thought they would be happy. I know I work them hard. I run myself into the ground keeping things at the level we're at. I don't understand what the issue is here.

"I like shit the way it is," Deacon says, and Dexter nods his head.

Fucking twins.

Donavan is quiet, taking it all in. I expected his support most of all.

I put my palm to my forehead. "Well, I don't, and you know exactly why. I don't need you to fight me on this. I need you to shape up and get with the program. This is a game changer that will be better for me and…"

"It's just sudden." Donavan finally opens his mouth.

Dexter and Deacon both remain quiet.

I narrow my eyes at them. "It's happening. End of discussion. Don't the three of you have clients or cases to be working on?" I don't always like being the hardass around here, but someone has to be, and I fit the role easily. I'm the big brother and it's always been up to me to set the example. My brothers have always looked up to me, so it really chaps my ass when they second guess my decision making. They should know I would never enter into a merger that wouldn't benefit both our family and the firm.

This firm is my baby; I would never just give it away.

I look around at them. "Look, you'll all have partner status and easier jobs. It's just a name change, that's all. Extra support. It's going to be fine, you'll see."

They all nod like they trust me—or maybe they've just given up—and file out of my office.

My line buzzes. It's Quinn. "Ms. Reynolds is all settled in her office, sir."

"Thank you. Did she find everything to her liking?"

"I believe so."

"Good. Thanks."

I end the call and lean back in my chair, my thoughts drifting back to Tate Reynolds and those spiked heels she's wearing today.

Finishing off my drink, I think I'll go check in on her and see how she likes that view. I know I shouldn't, but the whiskey is loosening me up a little.

I can't help but hope this merger will give me more of what I need—time.

TATE

"DOWNSTAIRS on the third floor is the cafeteria and the main supply room, but we also have a small break room and storage closet on this floor. The best part of the whole building is the roof deck. Follow me."

Quinn leads me to the most gorgeous scene I've ever laid eyes on. Clear as day I can see a panoramic view of Lake Michigan. The water is beautiful. I could stand up here forever, watching all the boats and just gazing at the blueish green that stretches to the horizon. A few buildings away I see a rooftop botanical garden.

"Perfect, right?"

I nod at Quinn and continue taking in the breathtaking view, falling in love with the scenery.

"Wait until you get to your office. You can see the lake and part of the park." Her dark brows wiggle.

Quinn is pretty with soft feminine features. Peach-colored cheeks, green eyes, and auburn hair. She's dressed in a dark green skirt and jacket combination that really pops with her pale skin. I hope she's someone I can grab lunch with during my time here. She's friendly, and I like her style.

I've never been to Chicago until this trip, but I can see how people love the place. I've heard the food is amazing and I can't wait to try out a few different restaurants.

We go back down so she can show me to my office. The view is better than I imagined. My office is huge and located in the corner with floor-to-ceiling windows. Decker has outdone himself. I was expecting him to shove me in a closet like Harry Potter just for the hell of it. He strikes me as the type. The kind of man who is an asshole just because he can be. I have a desk that's much larger than I'll ever need. It also has a sitting area that overlooks part of the park and Lake Michigan.

Maybe I could get used to this place after all.

"I'll be doubling as your assistant until one is assigned to you. If you need to reach me, I'm line four. If there is anything I can get you, just give me a buzz. Coffee. Whatever you need, I'm at your disposal."

"Thank you." The door closes behind her, and I get my laptop set up and arrange things the way I want them on the desk. I shoot my assistant in Dallas an email. Quinn is nice but I'm used to Danelle. We already have a system in place and she just gets me.

Danelle,

I need a list of touristy things to do in Chicago.

Preferably on the weekend. Throw in some good places to eat too. Also go through my contacts and see if I have any friends living in the city I could set up lunch with. I need my favorite black pants and those snakeskin heels...the ones that give me three inches in height. Overnight them to me, please.

I'm attaching the contact information for an assistant at this firm. Please see that you get her a cheat sheet to make my time here easier.

Thanks so much!

Tate Reynolds, Senior Associate

The Hunter Group

AFTER I HIT SEND, the door to my office swings open. I glance up from my computer screen and Decker Collins strolls in like he's the king of the castle. Just like him to show up and shit on my parade just as I start to like the place. I guess, technically, he is the king, but his arrogance is unsettling. The cocky jerk smirks at me again. He does that a lot and the sad part is deep down I'm starting to enjoy it.

"Didn't get to give you a tour. Thought I'd stop by and make sure Quinn got you settled in okay and that everything is to your liking. I'll set you up with your own assistant as soon as I find someone capable of filling the position." Why does it sound so sexual when he says filling the position? And why am I squirming in my seat as he speaks? This is ridiculous.

I lick my lips and feel parched all of a sudden. I'm sure my dry mouth has nothing to do with the sexy bastard standing in my office. "Thank you. The view is spectacular. Yours must be amazing if you gave me this one."

"Actually…" He strolls casually to the window and gazes at the picture-perfect scene. "This one's my favorite. It used to be mine."

Why would he give up his favorite office?

"I prefer being closer to the elevator." He answers before I can respond as though he can read my thoughts.

Who the hell factors proximity to the elevator to choose an office? Damn. I'm anal and not even that bad. I wonder if he has some sort of complex. I bet he's a time management freak and clocks himself in the damn pisser. He probably counts how many steps it is from his office to the front door of the building and tries to shave off a few seconds every day.

Poking fun at his routine sets my mind at ease.

I wish he'd quit grinning at me.

My brow lifts into an arch. "The elevator? You moved offices to be closer to the elevator?"

"Yup." He pops the P.

I sense there's more he isn't sharing with me. Reading men is one of my talents. It has allowed me to be successful at the ripe old age of twenty-eight. I credit the ability to growing up with brothers who loved to hold shit in and never wanted to share their feelings.

Being surrounded by their friends made it easy for me to pick up on men's social cues.

He pulls away from the window and comes toward my desk. The man stalks toward me like a lion ready to pounce on his next meal. I watch with fascination as he pushes the sleeves of his shirt up, revealing his muscular forearms. I've always found men's arms to be sexy.

Decker's are up there close to a ten. Who am I kidding? They're perfect like the rest of him. Nothing but corded muscle and rough sinew, yet tanned and smooth like he actually uses lotion. A few veins run from under his sleeves and snake down to his wrists.

He glances at his Rolex. I expected an Apple watch. I'm impressed to see some men are still old fashioned in that sense. Everyone is so plugged into their devices. It's the first endearing quality I've noticed about the man.

"I thought we could meet up for drinks later. We didn't get off to a great start."

"You stole my cab yesterday, left me in the rain with my papers—talked all this shit, and now you want to have drinks?" Wow, I should shut up, but I guess that'd been building at the back of my mind.

Decker grins—the most facetious grin I've ever seen in my life—like he relishes the conflict and wants to verbally spar. "First, I offered to help pick up your papers and you declined. Second, this is business only. No pleasure involved." He leans across my desk and my heart rate speeds up tenfold. "Pencil me in on your calendar. It's not a request." He taps the empty square in front of me.

My breath catches in my throat at his close proximity. I need to make a note to keep him at arm's length at all times. If he gets much closer, my brain might shut down.

"Um…" My voice comes out in a sultry whisper that's highly inappropriate but I can't stop it.

Decker gets up and starts to the door. "I don't know how you do things down in Texas, but here in Chicago, *sweetheart*, we do business over drinks." He mocks my accent by drawing out his words in an exaggerated southern drawl.

Before I can turn him down, the door shuts behind him.

I roll my eyes and sink back in my chair, nibbling the tip of my fingernail as I look down at my desk.

The blank space on my calendar stares back, mocking me. I should stand him up, but Weston's voice harps in the back of my mind. This man shouldn't get under my skin, but he does. I can get the job done. Weston always tells me I'm the best he's got, so I need to believe it too. Grabbing my favorite pen, I mark drinks with Decker Collins into my schedule a little too roughly and ink bleeds on the paper, ruining my pretty penmanship.

It's not a date.

I skim the racks at Ikram, settling on a Narciso Rodriguez number. It's black with a white abstract pattern and something that can double as work attire. A pair of Dolce & Gabbana heels, and a new necklace and bracelet complete the look. Finally satisfied, I get everything boxed up and head out front to find a cab.

On the way back to my hotel I rack my brain trying to figure out what on earth we need to meet for drinks about. Anything Decker wants to discuss can be done at the office. Hell, he can do it on the phone if he wants.

The only thought running through my mind is he wants me there in person. The thought sends a shiver up my spine for two different reasons. One, maybe he's attracted to me and wants to get me drunk and do naughty things to me. Two, maybe he wants to actually discuss work and be an insufferable prick the entire time. Nothing good can come of this, yet I can't help but notice I just bought an entire new outfit I don't need, but it's perfect and I look hot as shit in it.

I shake my head as the cabbie pulls up to the curb and drops me in front of the hotel.

It's going to be a long night.

Later, as I get ready in my hotel room, I can't help but feel this is very much a date. I've analyzed this situation from front to back, replaying every word in my mind and every one of Decker's reactions and the inflection in his voice. He said it wasn't a date, and I don't want it to be because we work together. But still… despite all my reservations, I have that giddy feeling all girls get before a first date.

Butterflies flutter around in my stomach. I primp in the mirror touching up my makeup and taking my hair down. I run my fingers through the waves and spritz it with some hairspray. I look over my appearance and know I'm spending more time than I usually would for a business meeting. Apparently, a girl has to look good when going out for the night in a new city even if it is just for drinks with a colleague.

I'm doomed.

DECKER

I HOP out of the shower and wrap a towel around my waist. Water trickles down my torso as I stand at the sink to brush my teeth. I don't know why I'm making a big deal about going out for drinks with Tate. I only asked because I thought maybe it would loosen her up and help with the transition for the merger if I get to know her better. She can learn a little more about me in a more intimate setting while still keeping things neutral outside the office. I probably wouldn't have been such a prick to her the first time I met her if I knew I'd have to work with her.

Yeah, you would. Who are you kidding?

The only problem is from the moment I crashed into her on the sidewalk, I haven't been able to get her out of my head. Her cute accent. The fact she gives me shit right back as good as I dish it out. She's got—something. Gumption, maybe? Attitude? I just like the way she challenges me, both of us competing to be the dominant voice in the conversation. Nothing more.

So why the hell am I so damn nervous? This is not a damn date. I'm Decker Collins. I don't need to stick my dick in the company gene pool to get laid. I can fuck any eligible woman in Chicago I want. I have. I don't do relationships or the dating scene. My life doesn't allow for it. It's why arrangements like I had with Jessica are key. Tate doesn't strike me as the type of woman I could get away with just fucking occasionally mid-day in a hotel room. A woman like her doesn't even need a man, but I bet she still wants the fairytale romance all the same. All women want that shit, even if they act like they don't.

I hear the backdoor shut. Molly, my housekeeper, is here. Over the next several minutes I finish getting dressed in something a little more casual than the usual suit and tie I wear for work. I go with a pair of dark jeans and a grey fitted v-neck. I pocket my wallet and head to the kitchen to greet Molly.

She's been with me for years and does an excellent job keeping my household running efficiently. Her dark hair is swept back in a tight bun that rests neatly on her head. There are streaks of gray around her temples. She's already busying herself with dinner though I won't be around to eat it until later.

"Good evening, Miss Molly. Something smells good."

"I'm making chicken parm, a garden salad, and

cheesy garlic bread." The woman can cook anything. Her Italian is to die for. No one can top her in the kitchen.

"Sounds perfect. I have to go out, but I'll be back no later than nine."

"No worries. Take your time. I'll hold down the fort."

Molly is truly a godsend, and I don't know what I'd do without her. She's like family. I grab my keys off the hook and go into the garage and hop in the Audi.

TEN MINUTES LATE, I find Tate waiting for me in the lounge at The Violet Hour. I couldn't be the first one here, looking all desperate. The Violet Hour is known for its speakeasy vibe and their house bourbon. I've only been here a couple of times and forget about their no cell phone in the lounge rule and switch my phone to vibrate. I slip it back into my pocket when I see the sign. I grab a chair and slide it next to Tate's so we can talk privately away from the chatter at the bar.

I let the server know I'll have whatever Tate is having. She's dressed to kill in her black and white dress. Fuck me, she's even hotter than she was the previous two times we met. Her heels have sexy black leather straps that wrap around her ankles in an erotic fashion, and suddenly I feel way underdressed.

"Two Midnight Stingers," she says.

The bartender scurries off and a moment later returns with the drinks. The whole time he was away, I had to will myself not to stare at Tate in her goddamn dress.

Once the bartender is gone, I break the ice. "Enjoying the city?"

She regards me for a few long seconds, like she's plotting, trying to figure out my motivations for this little get together. "Undecided, but I do love the view from my office."

That's something I've noticed about her. She's always watching, observing, her mind always working, taking in information. When she mentions the view, I can't help but think how much I'm enjoying the view in front of me. "Is our office different from Dallas?"

"Not much." She takes a sip from her tumbler, eyeing me over the brim of her glass looking like an angel sent here to torture me. The glow of the candle illuminates her hair. "Remind me. How do you know Weston?"

I smile. "We went to law school together. After I gave up baseball to pursue law that is."

"You played for Illinois. I read about you."

"You did your homework. Only heard good things I hope." I'm impressed she went to the trouble. I can imagine the shit she came across on the gossip sites that call me a playboy.

"Maybe," she says as we both take a drink. "What was that like? The baseball?"

"Loved it. I lived for the game, but it was exhausting and a lot of hard work."

"If you could go back and do things differently… would you have pursued baseball instead of law?"

It's not the question I expect, and it catches me off guard for a second. I right the ship before she can tell something is off. "No. Part of me wonders what if, but things turned out good. I got to play ball for a while and things worked out." I made my peace with the choice I made a long time ago. I wouldn't trade the life I have today for anything in the world.

"You miss the recognition that came with it?" Her tongue darts out as she beams at me, tapping her nails on her glass in need of another drink.

"No. I didn't like the attention." I signal for a refill.

"Trying to get me drunk? Thought this was business." She wraps her red painted nails around her bourbon-filled glass.

Talking to Tate comes naturally. She's great at conversation and a good listener. I need to change the subject, though. She always just dives straight into the uncomfortable. Ignoring her comment, I say, "Enough about me. Tell me about you. You grew up in Texas?"

"I did. I have two older brothers who didn't mind me tagging along on their fishing and hunting trips."

"You fish and hunt?"

"I'm a southern girl. I can drink like a fish and swim like one too." She laughs, a real, genuine laugh this time.

"I see that. Bet you put the men in Dallas to shame."

She brings her rocks glass up toward her lips but lets it rest against her chin. "I do my best."

"Kicking ass and taking names?"

"Something like that. I keep them in line and crack the whip when I need to." There's a naughty sparkle in her eyes, but maybe it's the flame from the candle.

"You really as tough as Weston says? Or is he just talking shit?"

The corners of her lips curl up into a grin. "Oh, I imagine you'll find out soon enough, counselor."

I can't help but smile. Fuck, this woman is perfect.

She glances around the bar. "You bring all your colleagues here?"

I stroke my jaw. We're both playing with fire. "This is only my third time here. So, to answer your question, no."

"Just me, huh? Does that make me special?"

She's special all right. A damn temptress.

Her Cupid's bow lips curve upward forming a delicious smirk.

"You're something… I just haven't figured out what yet." Knocking back my drink, I place the empty tumbler on the table between us.

She finishes hers. Her fingers linger on the table, her red nails on display. I imagine them scratching down my back after I've peeled that dress from her.

I shake myself out of these thoughts. I should get going, but I can't seem to pull myself away from her.

The low lights, the proximity of our chairs, her cinnamon vanilla scent—it all mingles together, and I inch closer. I think the bourbon has gone straight to my dick and my brain is no longer able to function.

Tate licks her tempting red lips. Lips I want to kiss but know I shouldn't. Those gorgeous honey-brown eyes meet mine full of playfulness. I lean forward, determined to see if her mouth tastes as sweet as I imagine. This is it, the moment of truth. There's no coming back, but I'm determined to feel her lips on mine.

Her eyelashes flutter and she doesn't stop me. I lean in farther, our mouths just inches apart, close enough I can feel her breath play across my chin.

Fuck it.

I go for it. The one thing that could tank this deal, and one of the dumbest decisions I could possibly make.

My phone vibrates in my pocket.

I pull away and glance at my watch; I see it's already after nine. I lost track of the time. It's not hard to do with the gorgeous Tate Reynolds sitting next to me at the bar. Her eyes remain locked on mine the entire time, probably wondering what the fuck I'm doing. She lets out a small flustered sigh, but, other than that, her poker face remains.

When I pull my phone from my pocket and read the message, my heart damn near beats out of my chest. "Fuck. I gotta go."

Tate frowns, but tries to hide it almost immediately.

"Sorry." I slip money to the server for our drinks and head out of the bar.

We accomplished no work whatsoever. We didn't even discuss the merger.

I did learn one thing about myself, though.

I want Tate Reynolds—bad.

TATE

THINGS ARE weird the next day when I walk into the office. Quinn strolls by and says hello, nothing new there. I catch the other three Collins brothers brooding at me from their desks. They're not hard to miss. The whole office is made out of glass walls, so a ton of natural sunlight filters through the building.

I spot Decker at the end of the hall, so I start in his direction. I can't stop thinking about how close he was to my mouth last night, and how badly I wanted him to kiss me. It would've been a mistake, so I'd breathed easy when his phone rang.

The last thing I want is for things to be weird, but I'm drawn to him like a moth to a flame. He has a way about him that pulls me in like a tractor beam and turns me into a mindless buffoon. As soon as he spots me, he takes off in the other direction.

Just like all the men in your life, scared.

I suppose it's not a bad thing. I'm here to do one thing and one thing only—my job. I head to my office and pull out my highlighter. It's not hard to get lost in my work, and that's exactly what I plan to do. I need to go through the client lists of both firms and make sure there are no conflicts of interest, clients suing each other, etc. Anything I find must be resolved and signed off on by Weston. It's a shitload of work, but that's what Weston pays me for. I make it through a few lines of a contract before the words all jumble together and nothing makes sense. My brain can't process anything, and it's all because of the memory of Decker Collins' mouth inches from mine, hanging there, lingering.

I can't help but think about what it'd be like in my ear, whispering all kinds of dirty words about what he wanted to do to me. How he'd order me to get on my knees, with his hand gripping the back of my neck and pushing me down.

Goosebumps pebble all over my body and I shiver a little in the best kind of way at the thought. How am I supposed to get any work done knowing he's in the same proximity as me? He could barge into my office at any moment and I'd be helpless, a slave to him.

I have to get out of here for a bit.

It's almost lunch time so I gather up my paperwork and decide I can get more done in my hotel room for an hour with no distractions. I stop by Quinn's desk on my way and let her know I'm going to lunch.

As I head toward the elevator, Decker walks out of

his office and we nearly collide again. This time, he doesn't barrel over me with his shoulder. His eyes widen when he sees me, and the look on his face says he's warring with himself.

He starts to say something, but no words come out, and then he just walks past me.

"You're really gonna ghost me? Just like that?"

He freezes in his tracks, his Salvatore Ferragamo dress shoes squeaking on the tile as he stops. His hands ball into fists at his sides, then he slowly releases the tension from his body and turns around.

"Everything going okay?" He nods to the folder tucked under my arm.

"Yeah. Gonna head to the hotel and work during lunch. I can't get anything done in my office for some reason." I take a few steps toward him.

He looks like he wants to retreat, but quickly remembers his name is on the wall, and stands his ground.

I take another step closer. "We should talk about what happened last night."

"Funny, I was thinking we should do the exact opposite."

"Typical man," I say, before realizing I said it out loud.

Decker smirks at my response. "Now's not the time, *Tate*."

Why does he have to use my first name and keep things unprofessional? I'm trying to do the exact opposite. All I want to tell him is it's a good thing his phone rang before we made a mistake we both regretted. That way we can put last night behind us. "It's Ms. Reynolds." My words come out harsher than intended.

"Well, Ms. Reynolds." He takes a step closer to me. "*Now* is not the time. I'm busy and this is hardly the setting to have such a conversation." Sarcasm oozes from his tone as he mocks me in his most professional voice possible. I want to grab his tie and give it a yank, just to choke him a little bit, nothing serious.

"Well then, Mr. Collins. I guess I'll be on my way. I'll have work for you and Weston to review by tomorrow morning." I turn toward the elevator.

"Ms. Reynolds?"

I whip around. "Yes?"

He glances around to make sure the coast is clear, then lowers his voice. "Try not to think about me too much while you're reading those documents." The asshole winks and walks off.

Ugh! Fuck you, Decker Collins.

BACK AT THE HOTEL, I can't think of anything but Decker in his damn suit. It pisses me off even more because he told me not to think about him and it's all I can do. I have forty-five minutes to get some work done without the possibility of interruption and all I want to do is run my hand between my legs and pretend it's Decker's tongue.

I turn the TV on and crank up the volume, trying anything to create some white noise in the background to pull my thoughts back to work. Finally, I manage to get about ten pages highlighted with notes.

Only forty to go. No problem at all, Tate.

Even the voice in my head gives me shit.

It'll have to do. Usually, I would've had this work moved off my plate in the first hour I was at work. I don't know what I'm going to do about this whole Decker situation, but I need to fix it in a hurry. That's how I live my life, figuring out the problem and solving it.

Riding Decker like a bull is out of the question, so what can I possibly do? I tap my chin, trying to find a solution. Being efficient in my work is vital to my success. Maybe I can run everything through Weston, then he can discuss it with Decker, and cut the gorgeous, blue-eyed man out of the equation. Any face-to-face stuff I can punt to Quinn, have her run interference.

Then, I'll never have to see him, won't have to correspond with him, and I can finally focus. I solidify the plan in my brain. Now, I just need to execute it.

It'll be easier said than done, but all I can do is hope.

DECKER

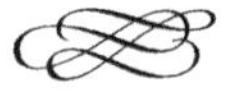

I SIT AT MY DESK, poring over my emails for the day. I prefer to knock them out as they come in, so nothing lingers that I can forget about. Fucking Tate and her smart mouth. I know I should go easier on her, try and smooth things over. She's just so—Tate. I'm used to confrontation, but she takes it to a whole other level. What the hell? Like I was just going to discuss almost kissing her right there in the hallway of the firm?

Having drinks with her in the bar was a bad idea. God, that fuck-me dress, and those hot-as-hell heels. I couldn't help myself. I'm only human.

Thank God my phone went off, and I had an excuse to get out of there. I sat up all night dealing with that message and now I'm sleep deprived and crankier than usual.

I pull up a Word doc and type out anything that

could go wrong by pursuing Tate. Making lists helps me compartmentalize and think things through.

Could ruin merger.

You can't date anyone right now.

Don't shit where you eat.

She has to leave for Dallas when this is over.

Typing it out helps me reason through the situation and get my thoughts organized. I was so close to kissing her I could practically taste the booze on her lips. The funny thing was, she didn't pull back, or lean into it. She just sat there, expecting it to happen. Wanting it to happen?

Fuck Weston for sending her here. She's driving me insane.

I hop up from the desk, feeling better about the situation after making my list. Now, all I have to do is keep my dick in check. About the time I walk through the door, the elevator dings and out steps the temptress from hell. My immediate reaction is to retreat back into my office until the coast is clear, but she catches me hesitating out of the corner of her eye. I can't look like some pussy and run away from her. There's no way in hell that will ever happen.

Shit.

She turns on her heel and heads right at me while glancing around to make sure the coast is clear. "Now seems like a good time to talk." She doesn't slow down as she barrels right past me with her color-coded files.

I appreciate how organized she is and at the same

time I want to smack her ass and send her right back out the door. Who the hell does she think she is barging into my office? Like she can't read my fucking name plastered everywhere.

I turn and glance at the door, debating if I should leave it open. I decide on open, that way if she starts in on me, I won't be tempted to grab her by the hair and kiss the breath from her lungs.

She stops in front of my desk and plops down on one of the chairs.

"Make yourself comfortable." Sarcasm oozes from my voice, hopefully some contempt too as I stroll around and sit down behind the desk, steepling my fingers.

"Nothing about our situation is comfortable. We need to remedy that right now."

"What'd you have in mind?" I can't help but smirk. I'm not used to someone else taking charge and steamrolling me in a conversation, but something about Tate doing it amuses me. I give her my best *I don't give a shit* look to let her know she's wasting my time.

She keeps on like she doesn't notice the way I'm speaking to her. "I've been thinking, maybe I just send everything to Weston and relay messages through Quinn. It'll put some distance between us."

I pretend to think it over, but really, I know the wait is killing her. I should agree to it. It's a reasonable plan, but I can't help myself. Torturing Tate Reynolds has apparently become my new favorite thing to do. I find myself wanting to disagree with her one-hundred percent of the time, just to see how she reacts.

"I don't think that's necessary. We're both professionals."

"It's not working, Decker."

"It's Mr. Collins. Let's keep things professional, shall we?"

Her jaw clenches and her face turns slightly pink. Not an embarrassed pink. It's a pissed-off pink, and it's perfect.

"*Mr.* Collins, it's not working."

"Working fine for me." I stand up as though that's the final word and start toward the door. "And that's really all that matters now, isn't it, *Ms.* Reynolds?"

She stands up and steps right in front of me.

I'm a head taller and I make it obvious I'm looking down my nose at her. "Anything else?"

She tosses the folder on my desk and crosses her arms over her chest. It pushes her tits up so her cleavage stares me in the face. Fuck, I can already feel my cock hardening.

She stands there, trying not to look pissed, but her breaths are shallow, and I can practically hear her heartbeat pounding. "We're not done here."

I look past her and fake a laugh. "Funny, I thought this was my office." I turn toward the lobby and point. "Oh look, there's my goddamn name on the wall."

Tate lets out an exasperated sigh. "Don't do this

alpha male bullshit. I'm trying to get this deal done and get out of your hair. Why are you being a prick?"

I lean down, close enough I can smell the cinnamon body wash she must use. "Because I'm not the one with the problem. I'm going on about my work fine. Why should I alter my schedule and routine just to accommodate you?"

I expect her to be taken aback, but she's not. She glares at me with a look that belongs in the fucking World Series of Poker. "Don't be an asshole. You might pull it off with other people, but I see right through it." She leans forward and gives me a better view of her breasts.

Fucking hell. Her tits are perfect, and now I'll have to pretend not to stare at her ass when she leaves, if she ever does.

I can't take this much longer. She's one remark away from getting bent over my desk. My palms are on the verge of twitching. I have to tone down this conversation and get her out of my office before I do something I'll definitely regret. I do my best to remove all sarcasm from my voice and give her an honest reply. "Look, I won't ask you to meet me outside work anymore. That was my fault. *This* is me being a professional and taking responsibility. Now, do your job, and we won't have any more problems. *But*, if I need to talk to you, I'm not going through Weston or chasing down Quinn in my own damn office. I'm busy as hell and I don't have the time. You're stuck with me while you're here. Deal with it."

She shakes her head, almost grinning, and picks up her file from the desk. "Men and their big egos," she mumbles as she walks out of the room.

Like a complete jackass, I can't let it go. "Not the only big thing around here, *sweetheart*."

I expect her to stop in her tracks, but she doesn't. No, Tate Reynolds heels clack on the floor as she sashays her ass in her skirt and stomps out of the office.

I'll be damned if it isn't a perfect ass too.

I stare at the door to my bathroom for a split-second. I'm going to have to rub one out or that woman is going to give me an aneurysm.

TATE

"You got that report for me yet? I don't see it in my inbox." Weston sighs into the phone.

"I'm working on it. You'll have it soon. Things are going great here."

"That's what I like to hear. Get me that report." The call goes dead, and I place the phone on the receiver.

It's been a little over two weeks since the confrontation in Decker's office, and despite the fact he didn't seem too enthusiastic about my plan, that's how everything has worked out. I know it's what I said I wanted, but now, something feels off about this whole situation. It's almost like I miss his sarcastic remarks.

I suppose it's been a good thing, though. Let things simmer down and get tempers in check. It's allowed me to get some work done and I'm ahead of schedule. I've met with a few of the larger clients and haven't found any causes for concern. Things have gone incredibly smooth and I hold out hope it'll last.

Conversations with Decker all happen through his assistant, text, or email. Maybe he's just been busy. He does run a giant law firm after all.

Regardless, I can never catch him in his office to go over the reports before I send them off to Weston. Quinn took a personal day today and I can't find Decker anywhere in the building. I went to the cafeteria, and the woman working the coffee bar said I just missed him. The thought of him fetching his own coffee does make me smile. With Quinn gone today, I suppose he has no choice.

I go back upstairs and he's still not in yet. I feel as though I'm the cat and he's the dang mouse. Like our roles are reversed. He should be chasing me. I shake my head and stop outside an office when I notice Dexter and Deacon have some kind of golf simulation set up, complete with a net and a TV screen. Come to think of it, I never see them doing any actual work. It's like they're hitching a ride off Decker and making boatloads of money in the process.

These two have given me the cold shoulder the entire time I've been here, and I think now is as good a time as any to fuck with them. "Is this how you spend time that should be used netting more billable hours? No wonder Decker called Weston." I make a tsk sound and interrupt their little game.

Dexter puffs out his chest. "Getting ready to take some prospective clients out on the course."

"Oh, I'm sure you'll land some absolute whales with that swing." I look at his pitiful stance and smirk at how he's holding the driver completely wrong.

Dexter does some little shimmy and questions his grip on the club by adjusting his hands. "Like you know anything about golf."

Deacon laughs and slaps his brother's chest. "I bet Tate handles balls with the best of them."

"Step aside boys. I'll show you how it's done once. It's five-hundred an hour for future lessons." I grab the club from Dexter's grip and take a practice swing. My skirt tightens on my legs, so I shimmy it up on over my knees.

"Can definitely handle the wood," Dexter says with a snicker.

Deacon shakes his head, but I laugh. I'm used to shit talking with men.

I line up my swing and drill the ball straight into the net. A virtual golf ball on the TV soars through the air straight down the fairway. I twirl the club in my hands then flip it on the ground at their feet.

They both stand there with their mouths wide open.

"Run your mouth some more, boys."

"Maybe I should be sending Tate to play a few holes with the Branson brothers." Decker steps under the door frame.

My stomach coils up like a spring and goosebumps

pebble down my arms at the sound of his voice. I look over and he's leaning in the doorway watching me. He's wearing gray slacks with a white button down. His tie is loosened around the collar and his hair is messy like he's been running his fingers through it.

My cheeks tingle as he stares me down. "Wouldn't want clients leaving when I kick their ass." I start toward the door.

Decker moves so I can exit. He follows but can't see the satisfied smile on my face. There's something about him walking after me that sets the world right.

"You'd let them win, *sweetheart.*"

I spin around. The way the term of endearment rolls off his tongue grates on my nerves, and judging by the wicked glint in his eyes, he knows it.

"I never let anyone else win in life or the courtroom."

"You'd let them win if I told you to." He smirks. "I hear you've been looking for me."

"I need you to take a look at something before I send it off to Weston. He's already irritated I haven't sent it yet. I get the feeling you've been avoiding me. Care to tell me why?"

"Ohh, Tate." He mocks me with his tone. "I've just been busy, you know? Running a law firm. Sorry I wasn't here to hold your hand the past few weeks."

"If any hand holding were needed, I think we know it'd be me holding yours."

"If only that were true."

We round a corner where no one can see and he grabs my hand, rubbing his fingers over my knuckles in a lazy pattern. I can't help but imagine his fingers touching me elsewhere. Heat blooms across my chest and funnels down between my legs at the thought of Decker taking me into my office and doing all the dirty things I've thought about.

"Where's this report you're so bent out of shape over?"

"On my desk." I smile at him and sway my hips as I walk over to retrieve it. I start to tease him but think better of it. I grab the accordion folder and hand it off to him.

"I'll get this back to you Monday morning."

"Good."

He pins me with his gaze, and we have a mini staring contest before he finally blinks. I warned him, I never let anyone win.

He lingers at the door and finally says, "What are you up to this weekend?"

"Dinner and a show with a friend."

The way his jaw ticks at the fact it might be a man sends a thrill of pleasure through me. I shouldn't toy with him, but I can't help myself. There's no way I'm telling him I'm meeting up with Alexis, a married mother of two. He can stew on it.

"Holy shit, look at you, girl," says Alexis as I walk toward her in the hotel lobby. "What's it been? Five years?"

I squint. "More like seven. I still can't believe you went and got married and started having babies. We had a plan."

Her grin widens. "Plans change. One day you'll meet your Tucker."

"That man is one of a kind. I'll give you that. If I didn't love you so much, I might have tried to steal him away."

Her arm goes around my neck, pulling me in for a tight squeeze.

"Oomph. You're choking me."

She releases me from her death grip. "Sorry. I'm just so happy you're in town. How long are you here for?"

"However long I'm needed."

"Well, I hope it's a long time. Anyway, Tucker is with the girls for the evening. I thought maybe we could get to the club a little early for a few drinks and an appetizer before the show starts."

"Sounds perfect."

We grab a cab to a place called Lazy Bird. It's tucked away in the basement of The Hoxton Hotel. It has a bit of the same speakeasy vibe as The Violet Hour, the place Decker almost kissed me. I wonder to myself what he's doing this weekend besides working on that report.

We're too early for the live music, but we'll get

enough of that when we see *West Side Story* later at the Civic Opera House. It's not too crowded and the atmosphere is laid back and friendly. Alexis orders us a couple of Blackthorns, a house drink made with Irish whiskey. It's a bit malty but goes down smooth.

Alexis and I grew up together but went our separate ways after high school. I pursued law and she earned her teaching degree. She tucks her strawberry, bobbed hair behind her ear and sips on her drink. "Tell me everything. Work, relationships, spill the tea, bitch."

"There's not much to tell, really."

"Puhlease. I've spent all my free time with the girls for the past five years. I need some adult talk."

"Honestly, I work a lot for one of the most prestigious law firms in the country. It's my dream job. I have a fabulous apartment in Dallas. I'm happy."

"And… you're still single? Tell me the juicy bits. I want to live vicariously through you."

"Yup. Single and not so ready to mingle." I gaze lazily around the room taking note of the décor. There's an old fireman's map of the city hanging on the wall.

"Why not? You're a total catch."

I swallow my drink quickly. "I don't need a man to be happy. I have B.O.B."

"Who's he?"

I can't stop laughing. "Battery operated boyfriend."

Her brows go up. "Oh."

"Don't you…"

"God no. Tucker would have a stroke. He'd get jealous of the competition."

I snort and change the subject. "Tell me about the girls."

"Mags, Maggie is my oldest. She's my tomboy. She reminds me of you in ways. She loves sports and is looking forward to camp this summer. It's for soccer. Then there is my Bella bean. She was a preemie and still small for her age, but she has the loudest personality. Kid is always singing and making a spectacle of herself."

"She's just like you then." I grin.

"Totally." She laughs. "Drives her father crazy."

"I can't imagine living with two of you."

"Hilarious." We chit chat a bit more about her decision to return to work now that her girls are both in school. "What about you, though? Think you'll ever settle down and do the family thing?"

"Maybe for the right guy, if I ever meet him. But I love my work. The job I'm in town for is my big shot at making partner at the firm. Life's good the way it is. I work a lot. Don't have time to get involved with someone."

"You'll meet your Mr. Right. I know it."

"Mr. Right Hand." I wiggle my fingers at her, and she can't stop laughing. I shake my head and order another drink. I don't want to think about dating anyone at the moment.

DECKER

LOOKING at the time in the right-side corner of my computer screen, I should be long gone by now, but I'm late getting this report back to Tate. Weston wants biweekly reports of our status. I should've had it ready this morning, but my weekend got away from me. I expected Tate to be on my ass over it, but I've been too busy to cross paths with her. My morning was spent with one of my largest clients. Cole Miller owns a billion-dollar franchise of fitness centers and spas geared toward females, and there was an incident over the weekend. An employee snapped a photo of one of the patrons and posted it to their social media. They made derogatory comments, and the victim lawyered up. I've spent the majority of my day combing over the membership terms and agreement while waiting for him to get me a copy of his liability insurance policy.

The whole thing is a real shitstorm. He issued an

apology on behalf of the company, but people are out for blood. It's being tried in the court of Twitter and frontier justice is on the horizon. The post has been removed but there are screenshots floating around. I have my team sending cease and desist letters out to people posting about the gym. It's already getting nasty. Cole has a reputation for being a bit of a brawler and a player. He's a former MMA fighter and the media loves dragging his name through the gutter of every rag tag gossip mag and site.

I know how the guy feels; I've experienced their wrath before.

Picking the phone up, I dial my house. Molly picks up on the third ring. "Collins' residence."

I scrub a hand over my face. "I'm just wrapping things up here at the office. I should be home within the hour. Is she upset?" I didn't expect to be here so late and miss dinner tonight.

Molly's tone softens. "She's fine. She knows you're doing the best you can."

I groan internally and stare out at the Chicago skyline. The Willis Tower lights up. I wish things could be different. "Tell her I love her, and I'll be there as soon as I can."

"I will. Oh, there's a plate for you in the oven."

I grip the phone tighter. "Thanks, Molly." I end the call. Guilt eats at me, but some things can't be helped. I can't be two places at once.

Not needing to hurry any longer, I run the report

once more and get it ready to leave on Tate's desk so it will be waiting for her first thing in the morning.

I stick the file under my arm, grab my briefcase, and lock up for the night. I nod at Gene, one of our security officers as he does his sweep of the floor. "Night, Mr. Collins." He clicks his flashlight off.

"Has everyone gone home?"

"I believe so." He steps into the elevator and holds the door open. "Going down?"

"Not yet. Have to drop this off first." I motion toward him with the file in my hand.

The elevator door shuts, and I continue to Tate's office. As I near, I notice a soft glow of yellow light on the floor. If I were a coward, I'd leave the file on Quinn's desk with instructions for her to see Tate receives it first thing, but I'm no pussy. I can't go around avoiding her simply because I find her attractive.

Tapping my knuckles lightly on the heavy door, I wait for her to invite me in. The sound of her heels clacking across the floor grows louder as she approaches. My heartbeat kicks up a notch.

The door pulls open, and her eyes widen when she sees me.

"Mind if I come in?" I take a step forward, not bothering to wait for permission.

She steps back, opening the door wider to put more distance between us. "It's your building."

She looks much taller today, and I can't help but look at her feet to see what shoes she's wearing. They're snakeskin, and she looks hot as fuck in them. I drop the file on her desk and my briefcase in one of the chairs.

"Wh-what are you doing?"

"Going over the report. I made a few notes and I'm busy tomorrow. Have a big case developing."

"No need. I took care of it. In the future if you say you'll have a report on my desk in the morning, I expect it to be on time."

"Is that so?"

Tate doesn't respond. She stands there, fuming.

I stroke my beard, amused. "I don't need you riding me, sweetheart."

"Listen up, *sweetheart*." She takes a few steps toward me and her eyes flash with irritation.

I don't know whether to be intimidated or turned on.

Tate puts both hands on her hips. "If I were riding you, you'd damn sure know it."

My teeth clench. The thought of her straddling me plays front and center in my mind. She'd be in nothing but those fuck-me stilettos. Her hair would tumble down her back while she bounced on my thighs, grinding on my cock, my fingers biting the curves of her hips. It would culminate with her bow-shaped lips forming a perfect O while she comes.

"That a promise?" My gaze rakes over her body, taking her in as she stares me down. She's wearing a yellow skirt that's brighter than the sun, her tanned thighs peeking out the bottom. The top two buttons of her blouse are undone providing a glimpse of dark lace underneath. With every breath she takes, her breasts expand and contract and I don't know how much more of this shit I can take.

I cross the room in three long strides. Grabbing her face between my palms, I look into her eyes ready to get lost in them. Those tempting red lips part, and her mocha-scented breath wafts over me. Tate leans in, and my hard cock brushes up against her stomach. The smell of her perfume invades my nose, and all I can think about is claiming her mouth, until Weston's voice sounds in the dark recesses of my mind and tells me not to get involved or I'll blow more than just a load in my pants.

I mentally curse Weston Hunter for sending Tate Reynolds here to torture me.

Dropping my hands, I pull away as my pulse hammers in my ears.

"This can't happen." I storm toward the door not looking back and suck in a deep breath. I'm losing my goddamn mind.

Fuck, this woman is impossible to be near.

TATE

KICKING OFF MY HEELS, I don't care where they land. I unzip the back of my skirt allowing it to drop to the floor and pool at my feet as I hastily unbutton my top.

Goddamn Decker Collins.

I'm so turned on right now I can't see straight. I told myself I'd never let a man get me flustered, but that's exactly what I am. My heartbeat is still ringing in my ears after that shit he pulled a while ago at the office. Who does he think he is?

"Think you can play these games with me, Decker Collins?" I say to no one in particular as I fight with my blouse before finally yanking it over my head.

Screw him. I need to release this pent-up frustration. I'm wound up tight and I need an orgasm like an alcoholic needs a drink. That smug, freaking jerk. His face flashes to my mind and warmth spreads through my veins. Once my top is off, next goes the bra. I fan out on the bed. My fingers move at their own accord rubbing over one of my nipples, pretending it's Decker's tongue trailing lazy circles around it.

I sigh.

He has me all twisted up inside. Rolling over to the side of the bed, I bend down to my suitcase and my hand goes into a frenzy searching for the one thing that can alleviate this stress, B.O.B. Once he's in my grip, all feels right with the world again.

Nobody can get me off better than me.

I slide my panties down my legs and roll to my back. Visions of Decker filter through my memory, but it's not enough. I prop my phone up on the nightstand and pull his photo up online. It's a few years old and he's volunteering at some baseball thing for a charity group. Shirtless and squirting water in his mouth, his abs are on display, and the dark hair of his happy trail coming up from his pants sends a thrill through me. It's why I chose this picture. I stare at Decker in his gray sweats that hang low on his hips and show off the vee that points like an arrow straight down to his cock.

Sliding my vibrator between my thighs, the hum starts at a gentle pace, but increases with intensity as my hips arch. Back and forth, I slide my favorite toy through my slick folds pretending it's Decker who's touching me. I want to feel that stubble on his jaw scratch between my thighs as his tongue licks right where I need it to. I can practically smell his earthy scent as I stare harder at the picture, enjoying thoughts of his tense body pressing down on mine. My fantasy is nothing but him taking control and pleasuring me. I spread my legs farther apart and tease at my nipples with my free hand. A moan passes through my lips.

I'm getting close.

Grinding my hips up and down, I rub over my clit. It's absolute heaven. My orgasm starts to build and then my stupid screen cuts off to a call from a number I don't recognize.

Ugh!

I snatch my phone from the nightstand after all thoughts of an orgasm dissipate. I slide my thumb across the screen and yell, "What?"

"Tate?"

Shit. This can't be happening.

I clutch the phone to my chest and get all tingly at the sound. Decker fucking Collins. The current bane of my existence. He must be calling from his house phone. I can't even respond because I'm so out of breath and worked up.

"What the hell are you doing?"

I finally manage to compose myself after a few deep breaths. "None of your business," I say a little harsher than intended, but he makes me crazy.

"Why don't you call me back when you have your shit together."

The sound of his commanding voice does something to me. The man sets my blood on fire in the best and worst ways possible. Desire hums through every cell in my body.

Without thinking I say, “Don’t you dare hang up.” I can’t see him, but I know he smirks on the other end.

“Are you under the impression I’m obligated to take orders from you?”

“Yes.” Usually, the sound of his smartass professional voice drives me up the wall, but right now my body is all about it. I power my vibrator back on, knowing he can hear, but I don’t care. My body has temporarily overridden my brain.

“What the hell is that sound? Is that an electric toothbrush?”

“It’s my vibrator. I’m not on company time. You don’t get me all worked up then bounce. I have needs.”

There’s a moment of stunned silence. I picture him sitting there, absolutely flustered and it sends another pulse of electricity down to my clit. Then, I think of him processing this information and his cock growing hard in his pants. Something about it turns me on more than I’ve ever been turned on in my life.

“Jesus Christ.” After a few quick beats, Decker lowers his voice as if someone might hear and says, “Tate… we can’t do this.”

“Don’t be a little bitch. You started this up, *sweetheart*, and now you’re going to finish it.”

“It’s not appropriate.” His voice comes out on a groan and my pussy clenches at the sound.

“We’re way past appropriate. I’m two seconds away

from going to the nearest bar and finding someone who can take care of it if you can't." I let out a gasp as I hit a higher level of intensity on B.O.B.

"The fuck you will." His voice booms from the speaker on my phone.

Please don't stop talking, Decker.

"What the hell are you gonna do about it then?"

"You want to get off, *sweetheart*?" He draws out the last word.

I smirk. "What are you doing right now, Decker?" I close my eyes to picture whatever he's about to say. I want every damn detail he has to offer.

"I'm in my home office sunk down in my chair with my pants unzipped. My fist is wrapped around my cock. I'm thinking about how big it would look with your small hands wrapped around it."

Of course, his fantasy is me pleasuring him. I can't judge him too harshly for it. My thoughts are the exact same with the roles reversed. "Mmm." My teeth dig into my bottom lip. "Tell me what you would've done to me at the office if you hadn't walked out like a pussy."

"I would've shoved you up against the window and yanked your skirt up over your ass."

"Mmm, go on."

"Know what? Fuck your little script. Let me ask you something, Tate." His voice is so goddamn commanding I might come before he even asks the question.

"Okay."

"Can you feel my teeth nibbling at the shell of your ear and down your neck as I pull your panties aside?"

Holy fuck.

I like where this is headed, but he starts up again before I can even answer his question.

"Can you feel it when I slide a finger inside your tight little pussy?"

"Yes." My word comes out on a pant and I wonder if he even heard it.

A slight groan filters through the receiver and answers my question for me.

I close my eyes, focusing on nothing but the sound of his voice and the feel of my vibrator, gliding it back and forth, imagining his touch... his mouth... his thick cock.

"Can you feel my thumb rubbing your clit while my finger finds that spot deep inside you that nobody else has ever pleasured before?"

"God, Decker."

"Yeah, Tate, I know everything you want. You want my tongue on your pussy, the feel of my face brushing up against your thighs while you squeeze your legs around my head and come all over my mouth."

I might die. The orgasm is front and center and I'm doing everything I can to hold it back.

"Once you come all over my face, I'd bend you over my desk, spank your ass and fist your hair and make you beg for my cock inside you."

I don't know how much more of this I can take. I

find myself decreasing the intensity on B.O.B. just to make it last longer.

"I'm so fucking hard, Tate. You have no idea what you do to me. For the past few weeks all I've thought about is tasting that smartass mouth of yours and fucking you so hard you feel me inside you weeks later."

"Don't stop. Keep talking."

"I love that sassy little attitude of yours. It makes me want to fuck you even harder, until you finally submit."

His words send a shiver coursing down my spine to my toes. His voice is the sexiest sound in the world right now.

"What else?"

"Those fucking heels you had on tonight… I want you in nothing but those, down on your goddamn knees, begging for my cock in your mouth. I want that red lipstick you love smeared all over it as you take me into your throat. I want you gagging on my dick while I pull on your hair until I come in that pretty little mouth."

"More. Dirtier." I don't know if he can get much dirtier, but I can't help but want to see where he goes from here.

"Know what I'm going to do, Tate? I'm going to slip into your office first thing tomorrow morning and crawl under your desk. You won't know I'm there until I grip your thighs and shove my tongue in your hot cunt. While you're typing at your computer, you'll be fucking my mouth non-stop. You won't get off until I say you can and at the last second, I'll shove inside you so I can feel you come all over my dick."

I whimper, losing complete control at his filthy talk. My orgasm quakes through my body and my eyes roll back in my head, my legs thrashing on the sheets. My hips lift high off the bed and every muscle in my body spasms at the thought of Decker Collins under my desk tomorrow.

I already know he did that shit on purpose and I don't even care. It's all I'll think about tomorrow and I probably won't be able to concentrate on anything else.

"Did you just come?"

"Mhmm."

"Good." He groans out the word. "I'm close too."

I grin, fully sated… well almost. "How close are you?"

"So fucking close. Fuck." His voice is strained, and it might be the hottest thing I've ever heard in my life.

"I bet you look hot as fuck right now fisting your cock. If I was there, I'd run my tongue all the way up your shaft and lick the tip, just to get a sample." I can picture him now, snug in his leather chair, looking like the king of his castle, ready to come. "I'm so wet for you right now, Decker. You have no idea."

"So fucking close. Don't Stop. Keep going."

Then, I hear it. The slapping sound of his hand stroking his cock furiously through the phone. It sends another wave of shivers through my body and goosebumps pebble up and down my arms. I squirm on the bed, thinking about him pumping up and down on his dick while he thinks about me.

I smile at the thought and say, "Thanks for the orgasm, I feel much better now." I end the call and laugh into my pillow.

Decker tries to call me back and I send him to voicemail.

One day, he'll learn—I always win.

Always.

TATE

I HAVEN'T SEEN Decker since I walked in the building this morning. Part of me wants to give him a smug look of satisfaction and part of me is a little mortified at what I did last night. That's beside the point, though. Something else has come up.

One of my biggest clients in Austin, BankIt, emailed me a lawsuit that's been filed against them. They're a tech start up and developed a personal finance app that uses a proprietary algorithm to help people manage their stock portfolios. A disgruntled employee was let go six months ago and has since went to work for another tech outfit in Chicago, broke his non-compete, and handed the algorithm to his new employer.

To top it off, the company in Chicago is suing my client for stealing their intellectual property.

The best part—Donavan Collins signed the fucking thing.

I march toward Donavan's office. He's leaned back in his large office chair with a look of satisfaction plastered across his face and the phone to his ear.

I tap my knuckles twice on his glass door.

He motions for me to come in. "I need to call you back." He hangs up the phone. "How can I help you, Ms. Reynolds?"

I can't help but notice there's a hint of smugness when he says my name. Surely, he doesn't know the people he's suing are Hunter Group clients or he'd never have been stupid enough to bring this suit.

I take two large strides and drop a stapled set of legal documents on his desk. "You know about this lawsuit filed last week?"

He leans over and grins at the papers. "Of course, I do. My name's on them isn't it?"

"It needs to be dropped."

Donavan let's out the fakest laugh I've ever heard. "That's a good one."

"I'm not fucking with you. Squash it."

His eyes narrow. "Not gonna happen. This is one of my biggest clients. And why would I do that, anyway?"

"Because BankIt is a Hunter Group client and this is a clear conflict of interest. We can't merge the firms when we have clients suing each other."

Donavan leans back in his chair. "Well, perhaps you should talk to BankIt, and get them to settle the case so we can move forward."

This fucking guy.

"My client isn't settling this frivolous bullshit. Your guys stole the algorithm from a disgruntled employee and now you have the balls to pull this shit?"

"If you'd cared to read the suit, you'd know we have R&D records…"

I cut him off before he can finish. "I don't give a shit what evidence you've manufactured to build your case. I know these guys personally. I brought them to the firm. They're geniuses, much smarter than you and I. They've been working on this for years. It's their baby."

"Guess we'll have to see it play out in court, then." Donavan stands up like the meeting is over.

I step right in his face. "I want it dropped. I don't have time to deal with this bullshit. I know what you're doing."

"And what am I doing?"

"You're doing this to fuck with Decker and the merger."

"I'm doing this because I believe in the laws of a free market."

I shake my head. It's difficult not to laugh at how ridiculous he sounds. "You take this to court and I'm going to kick your ass so hard you feel my Jimmy Choos in your goddamn throat. And not because I'm better than you, which I am. But because your case has no merit. It's fucking laughable."

Donavan smirks. "Guess we'll see then, won't we?"

I turn on my heel and march out of his office.

Fucking Collins brothers.

DECKER

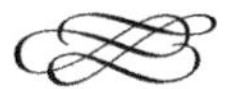

"Where the hell's my coffee?" I bark the question at an empty room when I get to the office and my usual cup isn't on my desk. "And where the fuck is Quinn?"

I pull up my schedule and my new emails. I smooth a palm over my head and cup the back of my neck, trying to rub the knot out of it. I didn't sleep for shit last night after that little stunt Tate pulled. The woman completely threw me off guard. I called to tell her I left my briefcase in her office. I wasn't prepared for the late-night phone sex that followed.

Fuck, I've never been so worked up in my life.

I've never met a soul like her. A woman who takes complete charge. Says what the fuck she means and takes whatever she wants. I was weak last night, and I never should've given in to the temptation. It took everything I had not to leave in the middle of the night, drive to her hotel, and fuck an apology out of her.

I head to the break room to get my own damn coffee still wondering where the hell my assistant is. I know she didn't call off and she's never late. On my way back to my office I pass Tate. She's talking to Brenda, Dexter's legal assistant. She smirks at me and shoots me a wink. It sends my blood boiling, knowing she got the best of me. Her casual attitude raises the hair on the back of my neck.

I try to ignore her and burn my lip on my coffee. Quinn steps off the elevator carrying a bag and steaming cup from a fancy bakery down the street. I start to ask why she's bringing me something she knows I won't eat when she hands it to Tate.

Goddamn it.

Not only is Tate fucking with my head, she's got my assistant running errands for her. Scowling, I retreat to my office. I arrive at my desk and realize I don't have my damn briefcase. It's still in Tate's office. Blowing on my coffee, I take another sip. I'll need the caffeine to make it through this shit show of a morning. Nothing is going my way, and everything is getting under my skin. I should've finished the job myself last night to alleviate some of this pent-up frustration, but I was too irritated to do a damn thing.

Donavan taps on my door and I motion him in.

He shuts the door behind him. "I gotta say this, so hear me out."

"Okay." I take a seat, and he pulls up a chair. He

sounds serious and Donavan isn't one to speak his mind unless he means it.

"This merger is a mistake. This firm was supposed to be about us. And you brought in your college pal and his associate is walking around here like she runs the damn place. She's fucking with my cases and has your assistant getting her breakfast. I just overheard her barking orders at Brenda, moving Dexter's schedule around. What the fuck, bro?"

Blood rushes to my face. It's one thing for me to be pissed at Tate, but I won't tolerate it from him. "Are you seriously wasting my time with this petty bullshit? I expect more from you."

"I've tried to refrain out of respect but this merger is a mistake."

"I don't need this." I push up from the chair and stalk out of my office.

I go to the one spot where I feel like I can breathe and clear my head. The one place I can get away from everyone.

I step out on the roof deck, and there she is. Her hair is down, and her curls blow with the breeze, wild and untamed just like her. Tate Reynolds is a damn force to be reckoned with and she knows it. I stand quietly and watch her as she stares out at the lake.

I start to turn back. I don't have the energy to spar with her right now but change my mind after the first step.

No. This is my spot. This is my goddamn firm, at least until the papers are signed.

Sensing my approach, she spins around and those passionate eyes of hers burn a hole in my chest.

Not this time. I hold her gaze. "This is my spot. How'd you find it?"

"Quinn showed it to me my first day. But you're a big boy. Didn't your parents teach you to share?"

I take a seat in one of the deck chairs. I wave my hand for her to join me.

Tate sits on another and reclines back.

I lean back as well, closing my eyes as sunshine beams down on us. "I have three brothers. I've had to share my entire life."

I feel her eyes on me and glance over in her direction.

"Everything?" She grins to insinuate we're talking about her.

"*Almost* everything." I make the point clear, though I'm certain Dexter and Deacon have pulled the twin switcharoo on women in the past. That's not my style.

"They don't like me much."

"It's not you they don't like. Well, the twins anyway. I hear you pissed off Donavan." I lean up, because the conversation has switched to a serious tone.

"He's acting like an idiot, but I can handle him."

"Yeah, I'm sure you can." I sigh. "They don't like change. They're used to doing whatever they want and maybe that's part of the problem. You intimidate them. And I've seen your work at The Hunter Group."

"Been reading up on me?"

"What kind of attorney would I be if I didn't? You're not the only one who knows how to research." I shoot her a playful grin. The more we talk the better I feel and the tension slips away.

"I'm not sorry about last night. You had it coming."

Pushing my sleeve up, I check the time and know I need to get back downstairs. "I'd love to stay here and tell you all the reasons you're wrong, but I have a meeting. Lunch, Friday?"

"That depends… is it for business or pleasure?"

"Pleasure." The word comes out before I can stop it.

"I'm not good enough to take to dinner?"

She never gives an inch, and I think that's what I enjoy most about her. I lick my lips, considering how to answer. "I have personal obligations in the evenings."

"Fucking hell, Decker. Don't tell me you have a girlfriend." She pushes up from the chair and turns her nose down at me. Her arms wrap around her waist and she looks away.

"I don't have a girlfriend. I just can't do most nights and it's not up for discussion. Just say yes."

"Fine. I'll have lunch with you Friday."

"Good. I'll send you the details after my meeting. I need my briefcase from your office. I left it in one of your chairs."

"I already sent it back with Quinn. I wouldn't be

stealing your assistant all the time if you'd find me one."

"I'll see what I can do." With that, I stand up and leave.

I have a date with Tate Reynolds. It's exciting and scares the shit out of me at the same time.

TATE

I CAN'T BELIEVE I agreed to lunch with Decker. I promised myself after the other night I wouldn't pursue my feelings any further, but he seemed so sincere when we were out on the roof deck I couldn't bring myself to say no. I know I'm bordering on inappropriate for the office with the sexy red dress and heels I'm wearing today but it's Friday and most places have casual Friday. I know I'm reaching for an excuse to wear it, but I want to look irresistible for him. I want the man to eat his heart out. I have a matching jacket over the top half, but come lunch that sucker is coming off.

I know I'm playing with fire and there's a possibility I could get burned but I'm going forward with our lunch date. It's just two people sharing a meal together, nothing more. But sweet lord the things his voice does to me.

Last night I thought about him while I touched myself in the shower.

I fiddle with my lipstick and tuck the tube back in my clutch.

Decker knocks on my door. "You ready? I made reservations."

"All set." I log out of my computer and set my email to away, so we won't be disturbed on our date by new messages coming through on my phone.

I can't help but notice Donavan glaring as we make our way out of the office. I flash him a smirk and keep walking. I should tell Decker about the bullshit suit and go straight over Donavan's head, but I don't want to ruin the lunch date. It's going to come up sometime soon, but not today.

I follow Decker into the elevator and the moment the door closes all the air pulls from my lungs. There's an electric current, some kind of magnetism between us. He stares ahead as we come to a stop on another floor. The elevator begins to fill, pushing me so close I can smell his cologne. I press into his side, unable to escape.

The elevator ride can't end soon enough. I need some physical distance from him.

We finally step through the door and I breathe a sigh of relief. After hailing a cab and a quick ride through downtown, we end up at a place called NoMi. The hostess seats us by a window overlooking Michigan Avenue. Decker's wearing a dark blue Tom Ford paired with a baby blue shirt. It makes his eyes pop against his tan skin and dark hair.

He does the honor of ordering for us while I freshen up in the ladies' room. You can tell a lot about a man by how he feeds you. The restaurant is gorgeous and the food smells amazing as I return to the table. He stands and pulls my chair out for me like a true gentleman. It's nice to see a northern city boy with some manners.

I sip my water and our Caesar salads arrive.

"Aren't you going to ask what I ordered you?"

"No. I want to be surprised."

"*That* surprises me."

I pause in the middle of stabbing my lettuce with my fork. "Why's that?"

"You seem to enjoy control."

"Any woman can be made submissive under the right circumstances." I shove my food in my mouth and the white dressing drips down my chin.

Decker stares right at my mouth, his eyes lingering on the sauce. I dab a napkin to my face, knowing what the image does to him after our conversation the other night.

"Oops. I'm a little messy."

He clears his throat and takes a gulp of water. "You're evil. You know that?"

"I've been told."

"You know a little about me. Tell me about you."

"Hmm. Well I grew up in a little rural Texas town.

When I'm not kicking ass in the courtroom, I take my nephews fishing."

His eyes roam my dress, all the way down to my shoes. "I still don't believe you fish."

"I won the junior bass tournament two years in a row."

He looks skeptical and shovels a few more bites of salad into his mouth.

"It's true. I even have one of those singing fish plaques to prove it."

"Don't tell me. It sings *Take Me to the River*."

"Liked *The Sopranos*, did you?" I grin.

"Guilty. I used to watch it on the way to away games in my baseball days."

"Figured you'd be too busy trying to pick up adoring fans."

"That too."

The waiter clears our salad plates and replaces them with New York strips.

I cut into the juicy meat. It's red in the middle. My dad always told me a real man knows how a steak should be cooked, and if he doesn't I should run for the hills. "Now I'm impressed."

"I didn't take you for a soup and salad kind of woman."

"Got that right," I say with a mouth full of steak.

"How old are your nephews?"

"Max is seven, Braxton is ten, and Camden's thirteen and girl crazy."

"Most boys are."

"Are you? You don't have a girlfriend… you say you don't date but this is a date."

"Can't give away all my secrets." He grins as he deflects the question about his personal life.

I want to push him further for more details, but he's still closed off. There's something he's hiding. I don't have any idea what it is, but it sets off all kinds of warning bells in my brain. I hope he doesn't have a closet full of crazy girlfriends or former fuck buddies. He could be a dominant and into the BDSM scene, but I don't see it. He's alpha but there's something I can't put my finger on. It bugs me. I'll have to spend more time feeling him out.

Our meal goes quickly, and as we walk back, Decker points out the different buildings to me. The Willis Tower, Trump Tower… to name a few.

I offer him a smile as we come to a stop outside the office building. "I had a good time." I actually mean what I said. It was really nice.

"Maybe we can do this again sometime?"

"I'd like that." I move to return to work when he grabs my hand, stopping me.

He spins me around quickly and I feel dizzy, like I'm on a carnival ride. He gazes at my lips and I part them wondering if he's finally going to kiss me. When his eyes meet mine, I can't read him. I should push him away and get back inside to work, but I can't. Because of one simple fact, despite how wrong it is and how much trouble I could get into—I want Decker Collins to kiss me. Right here in front of the office building, no matter who is watching, I want him to put his lips on mine and kiss me so hard my fingers and toes go numb.

I'm not a girl who sits around and waits for men to make a move, though. "Decker, if you're going to kiss me—just do it."

His smile broadens and he lets out a hoarse, "Fuck it." He grabs my face and plants his mouth firmly on mine. Our lips collide, mouths opening, and I invite him in. His tongue tastes like wine as he thrusts into my mouth, licking and swirling.

Finally, I pull away, breathless, and delirious. Decker Collins kissed me, and it was everything I had hoped it would be and more.

His fingers grip mine and he tugs me away from the building. With his free hand he hails us a cab.

My brows knit together. "What are you doing?"

"Fuck work. It can wait."

My pulse races as my heart pounds against my rib cage.

I get into the cab. Excitement courses through my veins.

Is he taking me home with him?

TATE

THE CAB COMES to a stop outside Wrigley Field.

Not what I expected, but Decker looks giddy like a little boy in a candy store. We slide out of the cab and he slips the driver a few bills. At admission he hands over his season tickets and escorts me to a suite. I settle into my seat and kick my heels off, tucking my legs underneath me.

Bringing my knuckles to his lips, he grazes them with a tender kiss. It's an intimate and sweet action that sparks some kind of hope that he's finally opening up to me. Maybe there really is more to him than just a cocky asshole who looks gorgeous in a suit.

Dropping my hand, he says, "I love my family and the law. This is the only other thing that compares." It seems as though he's choosing his words carefully.

That wall is still up, but I'll tear it down. I feel like I'm already halfway there.

"Baseball?"

Decker nods. "I sneak out here every chance I get." His face lights up as he stares out at the field below. These seats must cost him a fortune. We're only a few spots away from the owner's box. I don't know a lot about baseball, my brothers were more into hunting and football in Texas. I played soccer myself.

"You wanted to play here?"

"That was the dream. I grew up watching the Cubs. Andre Dawson, Ryne Sandberg, Mark Grace." He has this far off look in his eyes, and I wonder why he quit if he loved it so much. Everything I know about him says he should've ended up playing on the field we're staring at.

"What made you give it up?"

He pauses and takes a deep breath, collecting himself. "Life. I had what it took, but I knew I couldn't play forever and had to grow up sometime. The shelf-life of a baseball player isn't very long. You're always one injury away from having nothing."

His answer is a bullshit copout, but I don't call him on it. Nobody gives up on a dream that easily. They all know the risks and don't care. We're getting along and I'm enjoying myself, though. I'm not about to ruin this with an unnecessary argument.

He pulls out his phone and shoots a message to Quinn that we aren't coming back to the office. I don't know what she'll think but I don't really care.

Right now, everything is perfect. This day with

Decker is an unexpected but happy surprise. He's nothing like I thought when I first met him on the sidewalk. He's cocky but there's a sweet layer to him I'm slowly discovering. Weston told me he was a great guy. Maybe I was wrong to judge him so soon.

I put my shoes back on and excuse myself for a trip to the bathroom. When I return, he's chatting with some other men in suits.

"Tate." He motions me over and hands me a cup of beer. "This is Mikey Sullivan and Horace Martinez. They're clients at the firm and good friends."

"Nice to meet you." I extend my free hand.

"Tate's a temporary transplant at the firm. She's out of Dallas."

"I hope you keep her. I wouldn't mind meeting someone so beautiful in the courtroom."

Decker locks an arm around my hip in a possessive manner, but manages to keep a cordial, joking tone. "Careful, Mikey, she's lethal."

"I'd die happy." The man is attractive, but the way he looks at me all hungry like a wolf does nothing for me when I'm here with Decker.

On the inside, I'm rolling my eyes but, on the outside, I plaster on my beauty pageant smile and battle the urge to put him in his place. The last thing I want is to piss off one of Decker's clients when we're having a great time. "Excuse me, boys. I'm here to see asses in those tight baseball pants."

Decker releases my hip, and I move to the edge of

the box to watch more of the game, away from the boys and their likely misogynistic conversation. I know how men in suits talk and it's usually better for my career to just walk away.

I can hear Decker's conversation transpiring behind me. "Shit, you weren't kidding. I might be in love with your friend."

"Get in line. The whole office is in love with her."

Everyone but your brothers.

"You still owe me a round of drinks after I schooled you on the golf course," one of the men says to Decker.

"You promised me a rematch, but on my terms."

The man laughs. "No way am I getting on a baseball field with you."

Decker finally says, "I'll have my assistant call yours and we'll get those drinks. I need to get back."

They say their goodbyes and a moment later Decker's strong arm slides around my shoulders. His lips are at my ear. "Enjoying the game?"

I take a sip of stale Old Style beer. I think to myself only Cubs fans could enjoy this swill, but there's something alluring about a stale beer and a baseball game. "Mhmm."

His fingers bite into my shoulder with possession. It's sexy. I like seeing him in his element. He's a fierce lawyer but this is where his heart lies. Decker belongs on that field.

"Holy shit is that, Jose Balinger?"

"Didn't know you were a fan." Decker leans back, a

surprised look on his face. “Thought you weren’t really into baseball.”

“I’m not.” I take another drink of my beer. “It’s my nephew. The girl-crazy one.”

“I bet you’d be the best aunt in the world if you brought him an autographed ball.”

“Shut up.” I smack his chest nearly spilling my beer in the process.

He laughs and holds out a hand. “Come on, it’s almost the seventh inning stretch.”

“I haven’t the slightest clue what that means but okay.”

His hand wraps around mine after we discard our empty cups. As we walk down toward the dugout, his thumb strokes the inside of my wrist and every little touch leads me closer to temptation. His hands are magical and even a brush of his finger sends electricity shivering across my skin.

Decker let’s go of my hand and cups his hands around his mouth leaning forward over the dugout. “Hey JoJo!”

The player Camden is crazy about turns around and smiles at Decker. He jogs over and I can’t get past the fact the man my nephew worships is coming over to us. “Hey, Collins. What’s up?”

“This is my friend, Tate. Think you could get her a ball signed for her nephew?”

“No problemo.”

"Thanks. Just give me a call and I'll get it from you later."

I'm flabbergasted. I don't know why I'm being so silly and starstruck, but I am.

"It's that easy for you, huh?"

"We played together in college."

I wonder if it's bittersweet for Decker, but he doesn't seem sad about it.

"I'd get him a ball right now, but they aren't allowed to sign during the games. Some MLB rule. I'll get it to you, though, so you can send it to your nephew."

"That's just—thank you." My face has to be pink. Camden is going to go insane.

Decker gets us a couple of hotdogs and we drink another beer while we watch the rest of the game. We're getting ready to leave the stadium when I remember I never turned my phone back on. The minute I power it on it lights up with notifications and a call comes through from Weston.

"I need to take this." I step off to the side and answer the call. "Hello."

"Where the hell are you? I've been trying to call you all afternoon."

"Um… I'm at a game."

"Baseball?" He sounds super pissed off. "I'm not fucking paying you to go to ballgames with Decker."

I clench my fist and suck in a breath as Decker shoots his brows up at me. I pray he doesn't hear the way Weston is talking to me through the phone.

"Listen, Weston. We're a week ahead of schedule."

"I don't give a fuck."

Decker definitely hears that part as it booms through my phone. "Let me talk to him." Decker reaches for my phone, but I step away so he's out of earshot.

"I have something I need to talk to you about on Monday."

"Oh, the BankIt lawsuit? Yeah, I would've expected to hear it from the attorney responsible for reviewing conflicts of interest."

Shit!

"I'm handling it."

"I fucking hope so." He hangs up.

I should take Weston chewing my ass out as a sign to put a stop to this flirtation brewing with Decker, but I don't. It makes me more determined to see where this leads. I always do what's right and I'm never selfish, but today I'm damn sure going to be.

Decker stands in front of me. "You've been working your ass off. Ignore him."

"I've been dealing with Weston for years. I'll be fine. I can fight my own battles." My chest heaves and Decker pulls me in close.

"I know you can." His mouth crashes down on mine, stealing my breath away. We kiss and the rest of the world melts away. In his arms I forget why I'm in Chicago and focus on kissing him back. As our tongues dance, his cock hardens against my stomach.

He pulls away. "Let's get out of here."

Decker whisks me toward a cab, and I feel drunk on this man. As soon as I slide into the seat, he's next to me firing off the address to my hotel to the driver.

"Why my hotel?"

He leans in close and moves my hair away from my ear. "Because, *sweetheart*, I'm going to peel this red dress off and do everything I said on the phone the other night."

My heart pounds in my chest and his hand moves to my upper thigh. His tongue darts out and licks the shell of my ear and his lips move to my throat.

Decker's other hand caresses my jaw, his thumb rubbing over my mouth. I suck his finger between my lips knowing what it does to him… painting the image he's been thinking about of me going down on my knees for him. If we had the privacy here, I'd unzip his pants and give him a preview.

Sliding his fingers further up my thigh, he teases at the apex where my pelvis and leg meets. "I know this pussy is wet for me." His voice is pure gravel.

We both know we're about to cross a line we can't come back from.

Arriving at the hotel, the ride up the elevator is torturous. All I want is to get him alone and hold him to his promise. I can already feel the wetness on my thighs. Decker stands behind me, his erection pressing against the center of my backside.

We get to my door and he shoves me up against it before I can unlock it. "This is coming off." He fingers the strap of my dress and I nod in response. "Where's your key?"

I dig around in my clutch for the plastic card frustrated with every second separating fantasy from reality. A bolt retracts, the door swings open, and I start to kick off my shoes when he shakes his head. "I want those on and this off." He moves to unzip my dress as the door sucks shut behind us.

My dress falls to my feet leaving me in my strapless red lace bra and matching panties.

"Fucking Christ." The way Decker stares at my body heats me up in ways I couldn't have imagined before now.

He starts unbuttoning his shirt.

I move toward him and grab a pillow off the sofa. I drop it down on the floor. "You. Couch. Now." I smirk and go down on my knees to the pillow.

Decker grins at me with those blue eyes hungry with desire. He does what I tell him but still manages to look powerful and in control as if he's amused. He sinks down on the sofa and spreads his legs apart.

I unzip his pants, eager to get my mouth on him and hear him moan. I grip his thick length over his boxer briefs and flutter my lashes, toying with him as I rub my fingers along his shaft. His eyes burn into mine.

The head of his cock pokes through the slit of his boxers and I kiss the tip.

He groans and fists my hair, giving it a gentle tug. "Put it in your mouth, Tate."

I flick my tongue out and swirl it around the crown, teasing him, drawing the process out in leisurely strokes and kisses. His grip tightens in my hair, so hard his knuckles dig against my scalp, and I smile to myself, loving the effect I have on him.

I give in and free him from the constraints of his boxers getting an eyeful of how thick he is.

Right when I'm about to take him in my mouth, his damn cell phone rings.

A sigh escapes his parted lips as his head drops back against the cushions in frustration.

I fall back on my calves while he digs the mood killer out of his pocket.

One glance at the screen and his entire demeanor changes. "I'm sorry. I have to take this."

"Decker Collins." He listens for a moment and his face pales. He flies up off the couch so fast he nearly barrels right over me. "I'll be right there."

His hands are a blur, furiously tucking everything back in his pants, then he zips them up. "I'm so sorry. I hate to do this right now, but I have to go. It's a family emergency."

"I understand." I move to grab my dress. "I can come with you." I clutch the thin material to my chest.

"No!" He snaps at me, harsher than he's ever been.

I flinch at the unexpected tone of his voice.

He rakes his fingers through his hair and takes a ragged breath, then holds a hand out at me. "I'm just—

I'm sorry, Tate. I didn't mean it to come out like that. You just can't."

I do my best to keep my composure. I've never heard him speak to me like that. It's one thing when he's being a prick or sarcastic. This was more. It was pure—I don't even know the right word for it. It wasn't anger. It was just a tone that suggested it wasn't up for discussion or debate, at all. Whatever it was, it socked me in my chest and knocked me speechless.

"I'll call you as soon as I can." The door slams shut with his departure and I'm not sure how I feel about what just transpired.

TATE

It's been days and I haven't heard from Decker. I tried to text him to make sure he was okay and never got a response. I did my best not to take it personally, but we had this wonderful date and things were going perfect. I thought maybe it was leading to something, but perhaps I was just caught up in the moment. It's past ten and he hasn't been in the office all morning. I'm not sure if something is really wrong or if he's avoiding me.

There's one thing I do know. I'm not putting any more effort in with a guy who clearly doesn't have his shit together. I'm a little surprised Weston is getting into bed with someone who seems so all over the damn place. I lied to my boss and feel shitty about it. I told Weston we were at the game with potential clients when I finally called him back. It wasn't a complete fib. There were clients there. I put my ass on the line and for what?

A little tonsil hockey and phone sex? I nearly snap my pen in half.

My line buzzes. It's Quinn. "I wanted to let you know Mr. Collins is in."

"Thank you."

I take my lunch in my office, trying to give Decker an opportunity to come to me, but so far, he hasn't shown his face. I'm pissed off and hurt. It's a bad combination for him. I guess I had him all wrong. I've had enough waiting and decide to say screw it. I close down my computer and strut down the hall.

I walk in and stare him down with my hands planted on my hips. He looks up from some paperwork and his mouth opens then shuts. I tap my foot as my anger reaches the boiling point. "Well?"

"Tate… this can't happen. And we aren't having this conversation right now."

"The hell we aren't."

"Lower your voice." He stands up and moves past me to shut the door.

The second it closes, I whirl around and start in on him. "What was that the other night? Where have you been? You couldn't even shoot me a courtesy text to say oh hey I'm alive don't worry? You said you'd call." I fold my arms over my chest.

"You were worried about me?" His gaze softens a little at my words.

It's an unexpected reaction, but I pinch my brows together. "I actually do have some business to discuss with you, but that's beside the point. I know you feel the same way, so quit fucking around."

"Don't do this to me right now. Just don't push this, please." He leans against the door.

"You're not getting off easy this time, Collins. Tell me right now. What. Do. You. Want. From. Me?"

"Fine. You know what I want?" He takes a step toward me with wild eyes. It's kind of hot and primal.

My pulse hammers and my breaths become shallow. "No, but I'm kind of digging you being all hot and pissed off. It makes me want to find out."

"Is that so?" He reaches behind him and locks the door after closing the blinds.

I nod, desperate for him to make a move. He's so close and the sexual tension radiating from his body is off the charts intense. Christ, when this man starts brooding my legs turn to Jello and my brain to mush.

He crosses the room and yanks me into his heaving chest. No more words pass between us. His mouth comes down hard on mine and it's game over. Everything fades away—where we are, all my thoughts, the BankIt lawsuit. His mouth is on mine and there's no way I could stop it, even if I wanted to.

Pawing at my skirt, he shoves it up my hips. He backs me over to his desk, and tugs my panties down to my ankles. A tingling sensation radiates from my clit, traverses my body, and threatens to blast out of my limbs.

I kick my panties off and sit on the edge of his desk.

Decker drops to his knees and buries his face between my thighs, licking and sucking everywhere but where I need him the most. He teases me, licking all around my legs at the edge of my pussy, but never making contact. Every nerve ending in my body fires at once and I'm already on the cusp of the greatest orgasm of my life.

I grip the edge of the desk as his facial scruff rubs my inner thigh. Threading my fingers through his dark hair, I give it a yank bringing his mouth closer to my pussy.

When he slides two fingers inside me, my head tilts back and I damn near lose it right there. Decker owns my body. I'm completely lost to him. His mouth hums on my clit while his fingers make a *come here* motion inside me, hitting all the right spots in rapid succession. In and out, his fingers glide into my tight center. I'm a ticking time bomb as he hits me in delicious strokes that have me near the edge of orgasmic bliss. I throw my head back once more, panting. Decker works my pussy better than any man ever has. That's for damn sure.

My muscles clench, tightening my legs around his face. I'm two seconds from coming all over his mouth.

Decker pulls back and I try to yank at his hair, drag his mouth back to me. It's no use. My limbs are puddles already, and he's too strong.

Decker smirks. "Oh no, *sweetheart.* The first time you come for me, it'll be on my cock."

I don't hate it quite so much this time when he calls me sweetheart. In fact, it's kind of hot.

"Is that so?"

Decker's brooding stare bores into me. He undoes his belt and unzips his pants. "You're goddamn right."

I'm not one to take orders in life or the bedroom, but fuck if I wouldn't follow Decker Collins off the edge of a cliff right now. He's so intense and commanding. Veins bulge on his neck and I can't help but notice the urgency with which he got his pants undone, like he couldn't live if he wasn't inside me as soon as possible. Even with his disheveled dress shirt on I can tell he has the body of a Greek god. He's nothing but corded muscle and rough sinew. Veins snake down his forearms as his pants and briefs hit the floor.

His cock springs free and wobbles in front of me before he fists it in his hand. Sweet lord, he's even thicker than I remembered from the hotel room.

My legs hook around his waist and I yank him closer to me.

He stares down at my pussy and slides the head of his cock back and forth over my clit.

I squirm and paw at the desk because it's damn near too much to handle all at once.

Decker smirks, knowing he's in total control of the situation, and slaps the head of his cock on top of my clit.

"Shit, Decker." My hands grip the edge of the desk even tighter.

"I love the way you say my name when you want me inside you."

Oh. My. God.

Decker glances around the room and I wonder what the fuck he's waiting for.

"You on the pill?"

I nod, emphatically. I'm tired of waiting.

"Good. I got checked out. I'm clean. I can show you…"

"Shut up and fuck me."

His lips curve up into a devilish grin. He hooks an arm around one of my legs and keeps me spread open as he slides the tip of his cock into my entrance. "Fuck." That's the only word that comes from his beautiful mouth as he fills my pussy. His eyes roll back slightly toward the ceiling, then fall back on me. The intense stare returns, and he leans down and moves his other hand to the back of my neck, angling my eyes up to him.

Pure possession washes over his face as he heats me to a million degrees on the inside with nothing but his stare. "This pussy is mine."

And you're done for, Tate.

There's something about the way his fingers dig into my skin, the way he looks at me, the way he moves—Decker Collins owns me and he damn well knows it.

I try to think of something sarcastic to say, something defiant, that will piss him off and make him take me to places I've never been before, but every thought in my mind vanishes as he pushes himself in and out of me.

His thighs slap against my ass, and I let out a whimper. Decker clamps a hand over my mouth and I bite his finger as he thrusts inside me. It wasn't meant to be sexual. I literally needed some reprieve from the intense feeling of his cock filling me to the brim. He's rock-solid and stretches me from the inside in the best possible way.

"Fuck, this pussy is tight."

God, his filthy mouth has me coming undone all over again. If he so much as brushes a finger over my clit, I'll combust.

I have to do something. Something to take my mind off what's happening, or I might just pass out. What's that trick they say guys do to make them last longer? Think about car engines or their grandma? Instead, my body instinctively tries to piss Decker Collins off, so he'll pound into me even harder. "Shut up and fuck me, Collins. You talk too much."

A sly grin spreads across his arrogant face, and his hands grip the tops of my thighs, holding me in place. He stares down where we're connected, and his hands spread me farther apart, so he can watch his cock going in and out of me.

I don't know why, but it's hot as all hell. My heartbeat redlines, higher than I thought possible, and all the intense nerve firings in my body amplify by a thousand.

The two of us move together in perfect harmony.

His hips speed up, until smacking sounds of wet flesh on flesh echo through the room.

His lips meet mine and our tongues intertwine, then he presses his forehead to mine so that our mouths are inches apart. I feel his labored breaths on my mouth, and I hear every little grunt that parts his lips.

Through his rough pants he says, "Can you taste your pussy on my mouth, *Tate*?"

Jesus, this man.

"Fuck, Decker." It's all I can think to say. My brain has passed the point of being able to have a meaningful conversation. And the way he said my name at the end of his question—it sends my pending orgasm front and center in my mind.

I dig my fingernails into his forearms like I'm holding on for dear life. "I'm so close."

"Me too." He grunts out his response as his hips go to warp speed. My head bounces back and forth and everything blurs at the force of his hips crashing into me.

The stems of my heels dig into the top of his ass, cutting into him with every thrust. He picks up the pace and I reach between us to circle my clit. My whole body quakes the second my finger hits my sensitive bundle of nerves, and the orgasm rolls through me in huge, uncontrolled waves. My thighs quiver and I gasp. My hands reach out, grasping for anything I can grab hold of. Fuzzy stars firework in front of my eyes and nothing but pure pleasure rips through my veins. Finally, my pussy clamps down on his cock.

It elicits a loud groan from deep in Decker's throat.

Right when I think the orgasm subsides, and my mind returns to a state of normalcy, Decker grunts—loud. It's primal and raw, like a caveman. He shoves his cock so far into me I think he hits places no man has ever been.

"Fuck… Tate…" His dick jerks inside me, and he lets loose.

I stare up at his face, trying to log every reaction in my long-term memory. Every groan, every wrinkle that forms as every muscle in his body contracts. Hot jets of come shoot into my pussy and it streams out the sides of his cock and runs down my inner thighs.

He convulses a few more times, until he's emptied himself, then slowly a satisfied smile spreads across his face. I can only imagine the ridiculous, cheesy grin I must be wearing as well. I'll never tell Decker Collins this, but it was by far the best sex I've ever had in my life. It wasn't even sex, it was an experience.

I've never even come close to coming that hard, not even at home with B.O.B.

Placing a gentle kiss on my lips, Decker slides his cock out of me, and I immediately miss the connection. Tiny beads of sweat roll down from his forehead when he pulls back.

I can feel his hot come trickling out of me, but I can't even be bothered to worry about it. The way he now looks at me, all soft and sweet, like he feels something for me—like he's a different man for a few brief seconds.

I like it.

We kiss again and then I lean back to gaze into his eyes, seeing him a bit differently than before.

"Was that so hard?" I ask.

"It's still hard."

I giggle at that and he helps me to my feet and leads me into his private bathroom. Decker grabs a washcloth and wipes his orgasm from my inner thighs, then leaves to give me a moment of privacy. I straighten my hair and dab at my skin with a tissue to get the smudged lipstick look off my face. My lips are swollen from kissing him, but other than that, there's no sign I've been freshly and properly fucked.

I exit the bathroom, and he grins while he fixes his desk and rearranges his files. I move toward him and kiss his cheek, wondering where this leaves us now.

Before I can ask, there's a knock at the door.

I'm on my way out so I unlock it and Decker walks up behind me with a hand on the small of my back.

The door swings open and a woman stands in front of it. I give her an uneasy smile and she shoots a daggered glare right at me. I look back at Decker, but he stares at her with utter confusion written on his face. Then it turns to mixed annoyance and surprise. He clearly knows her, but she doesn't look like an attorney. She doesn't even look like she belongs in the building.

She's wearing jeans, a t-shirt, and sneakers with her hair pulled up in a ponytail. Her arms fold over her chest, and she just stands there like it's a showdown in an old western movie.

Shit, it's his girlfriend. Or wife.

"Monica?" He says her name like he hasn't seen her in years and they just ran into each other at the mall.

Did she hear us? Who the hell is this lady?

DECKER

This can't be fucking happening. The world hates me.

My head is about to explode. I stare at the woman who changed the course of my life fourteen years ago. She doesn't look much different now than she did then. Big green eyes and pink lips—just like Jenny's.

I swallow—hard—as a million different emotions swarm through my body. Anger is front and center. I bite back a lot of what I want to say and go with the obvious. "What the fuck are you doing here?"

"Our daughter was in the hospital and you didn't think it was something I should know about? Why didn't you call?"

Tate whips around, hurt and confusion written on her face. "Daughter? Are you married?"

My jaw tightens and I narrow my eyes on Monica. She never fails to leave destruction in her wake. I put a hand on Tate's shoulder, wondering how I'll ever dig myself out of this one. Tate doesn't seem the type of person to wait idly until I can give her all the facts. She probably wants to kick me in the balls, and maybe even a few other things that would inflict maximum pain. I try to tell her with my eyes that I'm sorry, and all of this has a rational explanation. "I'll explain later. I promise." I gesture to Monica. "Right now, I need to talk to her in my office. I'm sorry."

Tate's expression falls and her face pales. I feel like an asshole, but she'll have to understand. Surely, she'll give me the benefit of the doubt. Monica shoots Tate a smug smile and saunters past her and into my office.

Tate stands there with a shocked expression on her face, waiting for an explanation I can't give her in this moment. I shoot her my best *I'm sorry* look once more and brush a finger along her jaw, then I close the door.

I turn to meet Monica's hateful sneer.

"Banging your secretary in your office now?"

I hold up a finger and glare daggers right at her. "Don't. It's none of your fucking business and she's not a secretary. Why are you here?" I stomp to my bar and pour a glass of whiskey. I need something to dull the pain in my chest from the way Tate looked at me while I closed the door. Why does life have to constantly fuck with me like this? Why couldn't I have two minutes to at least enjoy the fact I fucked Tate so hard she came all over my cock? In my office no less.

That's every man's fantasy rolled up into one, and Monica shows up unannounced and ruins everything.

I take a hard pull from the tumbler and close my eyes as the warm liquid glides down my throat. I open my eyes back up, hoping she'll be gone, and this is some sort of twisted dream, but no dice. "It's been fourteen years." I scoff, shaking my head. "Now you're here. Like you're entitled to barge into my office and demand information on a child you don't even know. Fuck that and fuck you."

Monica shuffles her feet and cocks a hip out, like she's entitled to be defiant in my goddamn building. "That's no way to talk to the mother of your child."

I slam the tumbler down on my desk and take two quick steps toward her before I catch myself. I would never lay hands on a woman, but this is the closest I've ever come to being angry enough. "You're not her mother. Don't feed me that bullshit. Dealing with manipulating assholes is what I do. You're out of your league." I pause and take a deep breath, trying my best to calm down and be the mature person in this situation. "Look, I stepped up to the plate. You stuck your hand out for money."

She starts to say something, and I cut her off, figuring the best way to get her out of my office is to just feed her the facts as quickly as possible, even though she doesn't deserve them. I have damage control to do with Tate and, for all I know, she could already be on a plane heading to DFW.

"Look, we thought she had appendicitis, but she didn't. You've never cared enough to show up before, so that's not why you're here. What is it? You need money? How much?" I take two strides behind my desk and open the drawer, looking for my checkbook. I know how the game is played.

"Wow, Decker. Is that how you really feel about me?" She sniffles and wipes at her crocodile tears.

I'm not falling for her shit. Maybe, I was a little harsh in the beginning because of the Tate situation. That isn't Monica's fault. But I still need to draw some boundaries, or she'll think she can show up whenever she wants, and that's not something I can tolerate.

"I came here hoping I could see her. I want to be a part of her life. I know I made mistakes, but you didn't make it easy on me. I didn't ask for any of this. I wasn't ready, but you were."

I scoff. "That's ridiculous, Monica. You think I was ready? I was terrified. I had the world in my hands. My dream was right there. All I had to do was reach out and take it, but you walked away." I pause, because as much as I want to shake the shit out of Monica right now, I'm being way too harsh. Back then, she was honest about everything, and a deal was made. Truth be told, she did me a favor. It still doesn't excuse her showing up unannounced like this.

Monica looks away and lets out a shaky breath.

"Look, just tell me what you really need and stop playing games. You've got me by the balls for another four years until she's eighteen. What will it cost? I know you don't want anything to do with Jenny. She's a good kid and doing great. If you want pictures or updates, I'll send them to you over email, if you're interested. But you can't show up in our lives. Just tell me how much you need." All I can focus on is wishing Monica would get the fuck out so I can go to Tate and explain it all. This isn't how I imagined telling her I'm a single father who's just trying to balance running a law office and a family.

Monica squares her shoulders and lifts her chin. "I—I want to move to San Diego. I met someone."

I reach for a pen. "Done. Is that it? I have shit to do."

"It's really that simple? You'll just give me the money and that's it?"

I put my empty glass on my desk and stalk toward her, getting up in her face. "I love Jenny more than anything in this world, and I'll do whatever it takes to keep her safe and as close to me as possible. You don't need to use it as leverage. We made a deal, and I plan to honor that deal. You agreed to have Jenny. I agreed to raise her on my own and take care of any financial needs of yours for not terminating the pregnancy. But you are not allowed to come into our lives. She's my child. *Mine*!" I jab my index finger into my chest.

Monica has no claim on her. She hasn't been there day in and day out making sure she was happy, healthy, and safe. I've been here. I'm a damn good father and Monica knows that. Maybe if I actually thought she wanted to be part of Jenny's life it could be up for discussion. I'd let Jenny make that decision. She's old enough now. But this surprise bullshit is unacceptable.

Monica buries her face in her hands and looks up at me with a sadness in her eyes. "Am I that bad? You think I'd hurt her?"

I stare back at her. I don't want to feel bad for her but in a way, I do, because she's the one who missed out. If she only knew the experiences she could have shared with Jenny, all the pure joy I've been able to feel. She's the best damn kid. She's just—perfect. Our daughter is good and caring. She's sweet and smart. So damn smart.

Contrary to what Monica probably thinks, I don't hate her as much as I wish I could. I soften my tone and put a hand on her shoulder.

She glances up to me with what looks like genuine tears.

"You're not a bad person. A little selfish, maybe." I grin, trying to lighten the mood. "You weren't ready to have a kid. and I can never fully repay you for doing what you did. I'll always be grateful for that, more than you can know." Without Monica, I wouldn't have Jenny. It's that simple. I owe her.

Monica tilts her head to the side and walks over to my bookcase and picks up a picture of Jenny. "She has your smile, you know? My eyes. You're in for it when she starts high school. I was boy crazy. If she's anything like me…" She trails off seeing my eyes darken.

Jenny is nothing like her.

"Right." She puts the frame back down, sensing she's getting a little too comfortable with things.

I start for the door to hold it open, hoping Monica will take the hint. "If you need money, just call and ask for it. You don't have to pretend. Just be who you are. But you staying away… that was your way of being a good mother because she didn't need you part time in her life, and I appreciate that."

Monica wanders her way toward the door, not fast enough for my liking, but making progress. "I didn't mean for things to be this way. I just…"

"I know." I give her a weak smile. "When are you planning on going?"

"In a week."

I rub my jaw and glance into the hallway, making my intentions even more clear that it's time for her to leave. "You have my number. Just call. I'll get you the money. But don't show up unannounced and make a scene. We'll have big problems if this happens again."

"Okay. Thanks, Decker."

"Don't mention it."

Monica finally leaves for what I hope is the last time ever. I meant what I said though, I'd pay anything to keep her away. Jenny doesn't need that bullshit in her life. I pour myself another drink and something black under the edge of my desk catches my eye. I bend down and grab the black scrap of lace. *Tate's panties.*

Fuck.

I shove them in my pocket. We need to talk. I pick

up my phone and buzz her office but there's no answer. Not good.

Maybe she's on the roof deck. That's the first place I decide to check.

When I get there, she's nowhere to be found. The woman isn't in her office or the cafeteria either. I catch Quinn coming out of the supply room. Her face is flushed but I don't bother asking why.

"Have you seen Tate?"

"Oh. Um she took off early. Said she wasn't feeling well. I think she was going back to her hotel, but she didn't really say. Just the impression I got."

"Thanks." I storm into my office and grab my keys and my cell phone.

TATE

I STARE at Decker's office door after it shuts in my face and I'm speechless. I can still feel the caress of his finger on my cheek. The touch of his lips on my neck and the fullness of him inside me.

Now, he possibly has a wife or girlfriend. He *definitely* has a daughter.

How did I not see this coming?

There were warning signs, but I was so caught up in my attraction I couldn't see them clearly. Or maybe I just didn't *want* to see them. I'd noticed a girl's picture in his office, but she looked like a teenager. The fact he was busy on nights and weekends was a dead giveaway.

I was stupid. I didn't want to see anything past his gorgeous blue eyes and the way he made my heart race just by staring at me or walking toward me a certain way. My head spins. I do the walk of shame to my office, feeling totally exposed. People go about their work like usual, but my paranoid mind runs a marathon, judging every glance or gesture as an assault on my conscience.

Finally, I arrive at my office and grab my bag. I can't be here right now. Who knows if that woman will make a scene. She clearly could sense what we were up to when she came through the door. She could probably smell the fresh sex in the air.

Quinn stops me before I get to the elevator. She puts a hand on my forearm in a comforting, motherly sort of way. I imagine that's the easiest way for her to get Decker's ass moving to get things done, so she does it to everyone. Or, maybe she's genuinely concerned about me. "You okay? You don't look so hot."

"I need to leave. Can you…" I can't even finish the sentence. I can't say his name right now.

She cuts me off. "Sure. Feel better."

I'm sure she knows. Assistants always know more than anyone thinks they do. It's part of their job; to anticipate future needs and make sure tasks are accomplished in a timely manner. Quinn seems more adept than most, so I have to hold back the embarrassment I feel in every molecule of my body as I try to get out of the office as soon as humanly possible.

I nod at her and step into the elevator feeling like everything is moving in slow motion. The back of my neck is clammy with sweat and my stomach tightens. Nausea washes through me and bile creeps up my throat. I feel like I might hurl. Decker Collins fooled me, but that man isn't going to get the best of me. No man has before, and he isn't going to be the first. I just need to get my shit together and focus. Take this afternoon to get a grip on myself, and then it'll be smooth sailing until I'm back in Dallas, kicking grown men's asses in the courtroom like I was born to do.

I walk aimlessly toward my hotel and stop off at a bar for a drink. I don't even know the name of the place, but it appears I'm not the only person having a terrible day. I glance at the man sitting on the barstool next to me. He grips his hair and his head hangs over his empty drink. There's a wedding band on the counter and a stack of divorce papers. Sucks to be him. I can relate, somewhat.

"What can I get you?" The bartender stops in front of me with a towel over his shoulder. He's wearing a black tank muscle shirt and his large biceps are covered in tattoos.

"Something hard, and pour this guy another." I hook my thumb toward the depressed man.

The bartender shoots me a wink. "Coming right up."

The man next to me looks up when his drink magically refills. "I didn't…"

"It's my treat." I hold up the rocks glass the bartender sets in front of me, toasting both of our defeats. Maybe tomorrow will improve both of our lives.

Highly unlikely, but it's important to stay positive.

"Thanks." His eyes are red and rimmed with tears.

Poor bastard. Someone did a number on him. I know the feeling intimately. Decker just fucked me in more ways than one.

I knock back the amber colored liquor and toss a hundred on the bar. "Tip yourself and get this guy a few more rounds."

I should go back to my hotel, but if Decker is looking for me, he'll show up there and I don't want to see his smug face. I need to think three steps ahead of him to get my mojo back. I can still feel his cock inside me, and it doesn't make this any easier. It's not going to make this helpless feeling go away. This feeling I told myself I'd never experience again, that I'd guard myself against until my dying breath. It's worse this time.

I honestly don't know if I've ever felt this way about another man, and it's insane. We don't even know each other that well. Clearly, considering he has a daughter, and maybe even a wife or girlfriend.

Stop it, Tate. This isn't helping.

I pull out my phone and call Alexis. "Hey. What are you and the girls up to?" I hear them squealing in the background and I smile.

"Not much, why?"

I swirl my glass around, watching the ice cubes clank against the glass. "Can I come over?"

"Sure. I'll text you the address."

"See you soon."

I give the bartender a nod, then turn to the man with

the divorce papers. I glance down then back at him. "Nowhere to go from here but up."

He holds up his glass with a knowing look as I back away and walk through the door.

I hail a cab and give the driver the address.

ALEXIS LIVES in a two-story brick home in a quiet neighborhood. She even has a white picket fence to round out the perfect suburban scenery. Part of me envies her. She has the American dream. A loving husband who only has eyes for her. Two beautiful kids. A nice home.

What do I have?

A hotel room, more work than I should be able to handle, and a prick who pulled the wool over my eyes. They say comparison is a thief of joy and it can be. I walk up the driveway and smile at the chalk hopscotch drawn on the sidewalk that leads to the front porch.

I don't even get to ring the doorbell before Alexis opens the bright red door and tugs me inside. The girls are in the middle of the living room. One is wearing a pink tutu and the other has on athletic shorts.

"Girls," their mother snaps to get their attention as they play tug of war with the video game controller. "Can you two stop for five seconds and say hello to my friend, Tate?"

They both look up at me. Each of them gives me a quick, "Hi," then they go back to what they were doing.

Alexis rolls her eyes. "Have kids, they said. It's fun." She grins at me and I laugh. "Let's go to the kitchen. I have wine."

"Perfect."

I have a seat at the breakfast bar while she gets glasses.

She places them on the counter, slides one over by the stem, and gives me a look.

"What?" I take a sip and play coy.

"Out with it. What happened?"

"Nothing." I shrug. "Can't I just want to see my friend?" I do my best to smile, but it doesn't work. Not even close.

"Bullshit. We may have been apart for a long-ass time but I'm still your friend and can sense when something is wrong."

I lick my lips and take a longer drink. I really should slow down or I'll end up drunk. With my luck, Weston will call, and I'll slur my words all over the place. I can't think of a more perfect ending to this ridiculous day.

"Tate." She grates my name out like she would with her kids.

I smirk and give her the *I don't want to talk about it, but I know you're going to make me* stare. "Fine. I met someone and he wasn't who I thought he was."

"What'd he do? I have two shovels and a plastic tarp

in the garage. We can bury him out back and plant flowers over his grave."

I laugh. I can always count on Alexis no matter how much time has passed. We've always just gotten one another. "He wasn't honest with me and it bit us both in the ass. I straight up asked the dude if he was involved with anyone and he told me no. I knew he was hiding something, but I couldn't put my finger on what. I overlooked all the warning signs and red flags and went with my heart. Turns out he has a kid and possibly a wife or girlfriend. She turned up outside his door right after we—" I glance around making sure the girls aren't around to hear me. "Well, use your imagination." I suck down the rest of my wine.

Alexis looks up at the corner of the ceiling, quietly contemplating the most embarrassing day of my life. "Well, that sucks." She takes a few more seconds to collect her thoughts. "Do you know for sure they're still together? Could it have been bad timing? Did he say what was going on?"

"Nope. He practically kicked me out and slammed the door in my face. What's left to say?" I grind my teeth, the rational part of my brain glad the wine glass is empty because I might down another one like I'm drinking at a college frat party.

Alexis stares at me long enough for it to be awkward. I can't tell if she's contemplating or if she's upset with me, though I can't imagine what I could have possibly done. "Do you like this guy?"

I sigh and lean back. "Thought I did."

"Then yes, there's a lot left to say. Did you give him a chance to explain?"

I don't like where this is headed and my face heats up. I say to her through my teeth, "No. I left the office and came here."

"Oh God, you work together?" She shakes her head in that motherly way, like she wants to scold both of us and put us in time out.

I want to get upset at it, but inside I'm looking at myself the same way. How could I fuck up so bad? How could I be so stupid? "Yup. At least until I go back to Dallas. Which I'm thinking should be sooner rather than later. I shouldn't have gotten involved."

"Probably so. The situation sounds complicated." She reaches out and squeezes my hand.

"Your girls are being quiet." I tilt my head toward the living room, trying anything to distract Alexis from the problem at hand. I think it's more to take my mind off what I feel and all the thoughts running through my brain. We both pause to listen.

Alexis crosses the kitchen and looks in on them. "All that fighting must have knocked them out. They're asleep."

I stand up, not wanting to wear out my welcome. "I should go. You should enjoy your quiet."

"Nonsense. Stay for dinner. I'm sure Tucker would love to see you."

I shake my head. “Next time,” I promise and give her a hug.

As I head toward the door, Alexis stops me. “I don’t want to sound condescending, so don’t take what I’m about to say that way.”

I step back and look her in the eyes. “Okay.”

“Maybe you should give him a chance to explain. At least five minutes. Maybe it’s just a misunderstanding, and your feelings and everything that’s going on are amplifying it into a bigger issue than it is. I say this as your friend and an outside observer looking in. I know I don’t have all the details, but I don’t think it could hurt, if you can manage it.”

I nod. “I’ll think about it.”

I mean what I say. I will definitely think about it. There’s only one problem. I don’t know if I want to give him a chance to explain, because a part of me just wants to see him, touch him again, and I’m afraid I might believe whatever he tells me, even if it’s not the truth.

TATE

THE CAB DROPS me back at the hotel. I'm exhausted. The doorman smiles at me but I don't have the energy to offer him one in return. It's been a hell of a day. I start toward the elevators when I see him.

Gotta be fucking kidding me.

Decker Collins is sunk down in one of the high-back cream-colored chairs turning his cell phone over in his hands. He hasn't noticed me, and I want to keep it that way. I fall into step with one of the bellboys pushing a luggage cart, praying I can avoid him.

I stupidly look back in his direction and those icy blues slam into me. My face heats.

"Tate!" He hops up, rushing toward me as I get into the elevator. I shake my head as the doors start to close.

At the last minute he squeezes in. "Just listen."

"I'm not discussing this with you in an elevator." I hiss the words in his general direction and stare at the ceiling. I can't look at him right now. He'll win me over, somehow, I just know he will. I can't allow that to happen.

Yes, he deserves a shot at an explanation, but later, after I've calmed down and can think rationally about the whole situation.

We arrive on my floor, and I step out hoping I can make it inside my room without him barging his way in.

It doesn't happen. The man is on my heels.

Part of me smiles on the inside at how insistent he's being, and that's exactly what scares me. Decker Collins has an ability to grind me down until I don't even recognize myself in the mirror. Until I'm acting like a giddy teenage girl with a crush on the quarterback.

I groan internally and unlock the door. There's no point in fighting him. He's determined to talk to me, and my mind is one big jumble of frayed wires and misfiring neurons.

Decker comes in behind me. His hair is disheveled, and he looks like shit. *Good.*

I kick my shoes off and place my bag on a chair.

"Will you look at me? Fuck, Tate. Let me explain." He reaches for one of my arms from behind.

I can't see him do it, but I can just feel it. There's no explanation for how two people can be in sync to each other's thoughts and actions this quickly, but I feel it with Decker, and I can't give in to it. I just can't.

I spin around and yank my arm back to avoid his touch. The touch that will have me melting in his arms like nothing ever happened. "There's nothing to say. You were right. We shouldn't have gotten involved. Now look at us." I wave an arm between us. "I didn't come to Chicago for this bullshit. I don't want it in my life."

He takes a step back and raises both his hands. "I owe you an explanation."

"No. Really. Please don't. I don't need to hear any lines or lies. You don't owe me anything, Decker. Okay, we had sex, and it was great. That's the end of it. No strings attached."

His face falls, just slightly. Not in a disappointed way. In a way that says he failed me. "I want to tell you everything, Tate."

"Decker." I let out a sigh.

His blue eyes plead with me and I don't know what to do. This is new territory for me. Why can't he just give me a day or two to process? What is it with men not being able to take a hint?

I do my best to avoid the way he looks at me, but it's impossible. It's excruciating, because I want him no matter what. I want his arms around me. I want him to comfort me and tell me whatever I want to hear that will make it all better.

I absolutely hate myself for feeling this way right now. It's like my heart is sitting on the chopping block, and I've just offered to have a knife plunged into it.

He grabs my hand.

I look away and stare off at the wall, knowing I

should yank my hand away from him, but I can't and it eats me up inside.

"I didn't lie to you. I'm not with anyone." He sighs, and stares right at me, like he can sense my apprehension. "I don't mean to make you uncomfortable right now." He lets go of my hand and backs away toward the door.

My eyes drift over to his. This wasn't how I expected him to react. I thought he'd say and do whatever he could to try to get in my head again.

"This was a mistake. I should've given you more time. I apologize. I just wanted you to know that nothing back there was what it seemed, and I want you to give me a chance to explain. Nothing more."

I nod to him, as if to say *thank you, and you can go now.*

"My schedule is full this week with that gym bullshit. And I know you need a few days to process things. But Saturday night. Come to dinner at my place. I'll cook and we can talk about it then. Please."

"I don't think…" I take a step back, trying to escape his pleading gaze.

His face tightens and his brows narrow in on me. "Stop thinking so damn much and just say yes. Seven pm. Saturday night. Say you'll come."

"If I say yes, will you leave me alone?"

He nods. "You won't hear from me all week unless it's work related."

"Fine. I'll come. But no bullshit. You'll give me the

truth. I deserve it, and my bullshit meter is off the charts. If I detect a hint of a lie, I'll be gone."

"Okay." He nods again.

"Now go. I need to be alone."

"Thank you. You won't regret it." He turns the knob, pushes the door open, and walks out of the room.

As the door closes, I stumble back against the wall. I need to tell him about the BankIt lawsuit, but I just can't bring myself to do it right now. I can't introduce even more tension into the situation. It's like the entire world crashes into my chest all at once. How does this man make me feel so helpless? So, not myself? My lungs constrict when I exhale, like I was holding my breath the entire time he was talking to me. It's so bad I don't know if I'm having a panic attack or hyperventilating. He's just so intense, and gorgeous, and forceful yet respectful and sweet at the same time. After a few moments, my breathing returns to normal.

If there's one thing I know, it's that I've never felt this way in my entire life, and I really hope my brain decides to act normal again before dinner on Saturday. I don't know if I can survive much more of this.

DECKER

"What are we doing here? You never do the shopping these days." Jenny raises her brows at me.

I can't help but smile any time I look at her. She's beautiful, smart, funny, and everything I want her to be and more. She really is the perfect daughter, which makes things easy for me as far as raising her goes. Things could've been a million times worse. We're a team, though. Always have been, and every day I wait for it to happen, for her to have a defiant streak, for us to grow apart. It never comes.

I grab a cart and pull up the ingredient list on my phone. I give Jenny a look that says *sorry*. It's been like this for about six weeks, me working crazy hours. Once this merger goes through, things will be different, and I'll be home every night for dinner.

"I told you. I'm making dinner and I invited a friend."

Jenny grins from ear-to-ear. "Oh, is this friend a girl?" She drags the word out in a singsong voice. She beams at me with the same green eyes her mother has. It takes my mind back to the moment in my office. The worst possible timing in the history of the universe.

I haven't heard from Monica since then, but I'm sure she'll be calling soon with her hand out. I'll happily cut her a damn check and send her on her way to wherever it is she said she's going. I've kept tabs on her over the years. Made sure she kept her distance from Jenny. Monica is, well, Monica. To her credit, she's never pretended to be anything she wasn't, for the most part. Her little act at the office was totally out of character and I wonder what brought it on.

I guess she does always seem to put on an act when she's asking for money. She never just comes out and says it. We have to go through the same song and dance. Maybe it's a defense mechanism and she's just embarrassed or ashamed.

Her showing up like that really did a number on me, though. Thank God Monica didn't come to the house. That's the only silver lining I can take away from the experience.

Jenny makes a show of clearing her throat to get my attention. "Well… Dad? Is it a woman?"

"Maybe." I smile thinking about Tate.

I kept my word and my distance all week. It was damn hard, and she made sure to look hot as fuck every single day too. Every time I sat at my desk, all I could do was think about fucking her on it. The way my thighs clapped against her ass, and the way she clamped down on my cock when she came.

I wouldn't have had time to pursue her this week, even if she'd given me a chance to. The firm representing the victim in the social media body shaming case played hardball, but I think we're going to be able to reach a settlement outside of court.

Jenny hooks an arm in mine as we slowly ease our way up the aisle. "So, what are you making?"

"Grandma's meatloaf."

Jenny's eyes dart up to mine. "Do you even know how to make it? Why don't you just have Molly do it?"

I grab a carton of eggs and put them in the top of the cart, thinking about when Jenny was a baby and small enough to sit in the same spot with her chubby little legs dangling through the holes. Seems like a lifetime ago. I shrug. "Tate's special."

Jenny unhooks her arm from mine and spins around, stopping us in the aisle. Her face lights up. "So it *is* a girl? Is she your girlfriend?"

I don't know if I like how excited she seems to be over this. I don't know what to think. Part of me thinks I was hasty to invite Tate over. I don't know if I should be bringing her to my house, introducing her to my little two-person ecosystem. The other part of me knows this is the best way to explain my life to her. To let her see the real me and not the uptight asshole Decker Collins who struts around the office making impossible demands of people. "No. Maybe. I don't know. What's with all the questions? Feel like I'm on The First 48."

"I'm just curious. You've never mentioned a woman before." She glances down one of the other aisles. "Any woman, for that matter."

I give her a playful punch on the shoulder. "Just help me with the list and stop acting so—girly."

Jenny laughs at that one. "Don't know if you know this, Dad, but I am a girl. And I'm in my formative years where I gush over romances and teen heartthrobs, so while this dinner takes place, I'll be deciding if I can 'ship' you two."

I stare at her like she's an alien from outer space, having no clue what the hell she's talking about. Finally, I shake my head to rid myself of whatever teenage jargon she's speaking. "Go see if you can find a can of breadcrumbs." Kid is too smart for her own good.

She runs off down another aisle to get them. I survive the rest of the trip without another sixty-question interrogation.

I GET busy banging around the kitchen with the pots and pans trying to figure out where Molly puts everything. I think my entire kitchen has been rearranged over the last month and a half, and I have no clue where anything is. It eats at me that I've grown so distant. It's like I don't even know my own house. Part of me, I think, worries about the fact it seems like I'm not needed at home. Like Jenny and Molly can get on without me.

It gnaws at my stomach. One day, I'm aware, Jenny will be out on her own, living by herself. But that day should be far off in the distance. I tell myself it will all go back to normal as soon as the merger is finalized.

Molly has been making all the meals around here and normally on the weekend all I have to do is order takeout or pop something from the freezer in the oven when I'm not working. I used to cook every night. I start chopping the onions and get the meat ready.

Jenny sits at the table with her homework spread out. She's working on an English paper. "How did you meet her?"

I stop dicing the onions, and I glance up at Jenny. "Work."

I spray my hands with cooking oil, so the meat won't stick to my fingers, and begin mixing everything together.

"She a lawyer too?"

I walk over and look at the blank screen on her laptop that's open next to her book. "Don't you have a paper to write?"

"Answer the question, Dad. Stop deflecting."

I'm being cross examined in my own home. I ignore her and set the timer on the oven and put the pan of meatloaf in. Next, I move on to peeling the potatoes.

"If you're not going to write anything, you wanna help with the corn?"

"Sure. I got writer's block anyway." She puts her stuff away then joins me at the sink to shuck the corn.

My eyes dart back and forth between our hands. This is perfect. I miss it so much. Us, together, making dinner. I don't normally turn into a sap, well, ever really. But something in this moment, thinking about all the time I've missed with her lately, it hits me all at once. "I miss this. I know I've been working a lot lately. I want more than just making it home in time to tell you goodnight."

Jenny glances up at me and smiles. "I know you'd be here if you could. And I'm glad you met someone. You deserve to have fun and be happy. I worry about you being lonely."

I nod, trying to keep my emotions in check. "I'm fine, slugger. That's why this merger is so important, though. It'll give me more time with you."

"You need a life too. When I'm at college I don't want you sitting here all alone and pathetic."

I laugh. "Don't worry about your old man. I'll be okay as long as you're happy. That's all that matters to me."

"And impressing this Tate girl." She grins. "Is she pretty?"

"Yeah, sweetie. She's pretty. You'll see." I shake my head and suck in a breath. Tate is a little fireball. The woman is something else. I can't remember ever feeling this way.

"How old is she?"

"Go set the table."

I glance at the clock on the stove. Damn, it's 6:45. She'll be here before everything is ready.

"Fine." Jenny rolls her eyes but smiles.

While she puts the plates out, she looks over. "Maybe you'll have time for me *and* to have a life, once the merger is done."

"That's the plan, but you always come first. You know that, right?" I turn on some water in the sink and scrub what I can of the dirty dishes so I don't have to deal with them later. Something my mother used to do while she was cooking. She said no one wants to go to bed with a dirty kitchen or wake up to one either.

I think she'd like Tate. My parents retired to Florida a few years ago.

I drain the water off the potatoes and Jenny gets out the mixer. She's always loved helping me in the kitchen, ever since she was a little girl.

"This is nice, Dad. I've missed your cooking. Molly is great and all, but nothing compares to yours."

I smile at her, but the guilt eats at me again.

In a few years she'll be off to college and I don't want her high school years to pass me by. I already feel like I blinked, and she went from baby to a young woman overnight. I absolutely cannot fuck up this merger.

I find myself thinking about something else too.

I want Jenny to like Tate. I'm not sure what I'll do if the two of them don't hit it off.

A knock sounds at the front door right as the corn is about to boil over.

"I'll get it." Jenny grins and grabs me by both shoulders like she's giving me a pep talk. "Don't be so nervous, slugger."

I laugh. That's what I always called her when she was a toddler and it stuck. I look around the room and pray this goes well. If it doesn't, I don't know if I can handle it.

TATE

THE WHOLE CAB ride to Decker's, my leg won't stop bouncing up and down. He stayed true to his promise and gave me space to think about things. I still don't know what to expect tonight. I'm a wreck. Will his kid be there? I've never been involved with a single dad before.

It's not a deal breaker for me, him having a kid, I'm just not experienced with this sort of thing. I clutch the wine bottle in my hand as the cab rolls to a stop outside a modern two-story home with sand-colored brick. It has beautiful curb appeal.

I pay the driver and start up the stone-lined walkway. I let out a breath and smooth my hand down the front of my black wrap dress, hoping I didn't overdo it. I have no idea how casual or formal this is supposed to be. I knock softly and think about chickening out for a minute when the door swings open. A tall, teenage girl stands before me wearing a grin that matches her father's. It has to be her.

"Hi. You must be Tate. I'm Jenny. Dad's in the kitchen." She holds her hand out to mine.

"Oh. Hi. Yes. Tate. That's me." I roll my eyes at myself for being a bumbling idiot.

"Here." She reaches for the wine. "I can take that."

"Err. Okay."

Did I just hand booze to his minor daughter?

"Follow me." She motions me inside, and I take in my surroundings. The foyer holds a small table housed under an oval mirror. There's a picture frame with a collage of Jenny's school photos in it. A delicious smell hits my nose. I recognize sautéed onions and garlic. We pass an open floor living and dining room area. There's a double staircase that goes up to the second level with a balcony that overlooks the downstairs. Beyond that is a home office, and I assume a bathroom.

We walk into the kitchen, and I giggle at Decker's apron. He scurries around the kitchen in a frenzy. God, he looks so—different. So domesticated. Cooking dinner, rushing around like everything has to be perfect; he's even more attractive than he already was, if that's possible.

"You came." The surprise is evident in his tone.

"You cook." I walk over to greet him and tug on the strings of his apron. "Do you clean too?"

"Dad cooks all the time," Jenny states eagerly. "He's a great cook." She smiles at me then looks up at Decker.

He gives her a look I could only classify as the *dad stare*.

Jenny takes the hint and starts for one of the bedrooms. "I'm going to go check my, umm, homework." She walks up another staircase off the side of the kitchen. Either she's being sweet and giving us a moment alone, or Decker used some coded message to tell her to get lost.

I take a step toward the island and inspect the meal he's preparing. "Didn't think I'd come?"

Decker leans over with his elbows on the counter. "There were doubts, but I'm glad you did. I just wanted you to get a look at the real me. I'm not always the person you see around the office."

I nod. "So this is the real you?"

"Yeah. My life's not as glamorous as you'd think."

I don't know if I'm ready to have a serious conversation with him yet, so I change the subject. "So, what are you cooking for me?"

He backs away from the counter a tad. "Best meatloaf in the world."

I scrunch up my nose. "I hate meatloaf."

"Seriously?"

"No. Actually I've never had it."

"You've never had meatloaf?" Jenny comes from behind me and appears at my side. She's returned wearing a sundress and her hair is swept back in a low-hanging ponytail. She's tall and lean like her father.

"Nope. What's in it?"

"Meat," they both say at the same time.

Decker stares at me for a few long moments, then cocks up an eyebrow. "You've really never had it?"

"Of course I've had meatloaf. I'm a southern girl. Don't be ridiculous."

We all laugh.

The three of us sit at the table. Decker is at the head; Jenny is to his right and I sit to his left.

They both stare at me, anxiously waiting for me to take a bite of this world's best meatloaf. It smells fantastic, but they've adorned it with a lofty title. I'll hate to crush their spirits if it doesn't live up to the hype. I'm nervous as all hell, the way they're both leaning in before I'm about to take a bite. It's not the greatest situation in the world, having two people stare at your mouth. Shit, what if I hate it? What if it's so bad I spit it out or gag?

Well, here goes nothing.

The meat is juicy and flavored with onions. I finally finish chewing and swallow.

Jenny nods like she's willing me to enjoy it.

"My mother's recipe," says Decker.

I look back and forth at both of them, doing my best to maintain a poker face. For some reason, teasing out my reaction is a lot of fun. They both look like they might come out of their chairs at the same time and shake me, demanding my opinion.

Finally, I smile really big. “My God, that’s good.”

They both turn and grin big cheesy smiles at each other. “Told you,” says Decker.

“You mean I told *you*,” says Jenny.

I can’t help but grin. This really is—nice. Jenny is a total sweetheart and Decker looks happier than I’ve ever seen him. We eat in a comfortable silence for a few minutes.

Before it turns awkward, I look up at Jenny. “So, what grade are you in?”

“Eighth.”

“Favorite subject?”

“Math.”

“Mine too.”

We talk a little more about her grades for a few minutes. When we all finish, Jenny helps her dad clear the table. I try to help but they both insist I’m a guest and not to touch anything.

“I have dessert.” Jenny brings a box of cupcakes out from a place called Sugar Bliss.

I peel back the wrapper and bite into the vanilla cake with chocolate frosting. “Wow. These are good.”

Decker gives his daughter a glass of milk and offers me coffee.

“I know, right? Dad prefers pie, but I told him cupcakes are the way to a girl’s heart.”

The fact she wants her dad to impress me with

cupcakes warms my heart. We sit around and talk a little while longer over dessert. After a few minutes, Jenny gives Decker a hug and a wink she doesn't think I see, then excuses herself to the bedroom. Decker and I move out onto the deck to talk about things.

It's the conversation I've been dreading. I have a suspicion our situation is about to get real, and fast.

DECKER REFILLS my coffee with a carafe he brought out from the kitchen.

I tease him, trying to lighten the mood a little. "Who knew the dirty-talking suit from the office was a good little housewife in disguise?"

He laughs as he sits, and we take in the view of Lake Michigan from his backyard. Not going to lie, it's absolutely gorgeous. The weather is perfect. It's hard to believe we went from such an awkward, intense moment in his office to this, all within a few days.

"I'm sorry I didn't tell you before. When it comes to Jenny, I do everything I can to keep her out of the public eye. I want her to grow up as normal as possible, and my past and my connections at the firm, well..." He trails off for a moment. "It complicates things."

I look over at him, glad I came tonight. Jenny's a sweet kid. I'm still conflicted inside, though. It's just too much information all at once, and I need to take things slow. I have a job to do, and so does Decker. He has two important jobs to do.

I glance around to make sure Jenny isn't eavesdropping on us somehow. "The woman at your office… Monica? Where does she fit into your life?"

Decker winces at the sound of her name, and his face sours like he just sniffed a bottle of vinegar. "That was just bad timing all around. She's been out of the picture a long time. Jenny doesn't know her, and Monica doesn't really want to know her, she just… it's complicated."

I set my coffee down. "I'm here, Decker. You asked me here to lay all this stuff out. Tell me what's so complicated about it."

He sighs. "I met Monica in college, at the height of my baseball career. We weren't even dating seriously. It wasn't a one-night stand, but it wasn't a relationship either. We just had a fling. Things progressed and she told me she was pregnant. I wasn't even sure if the baby was mine, but she swore there was no one else. She can be manipulative sometimes, but she's not a liar.

"Monica wasn't ready for a baby, and I could tell it was tough for her to break the news. I wasn't ready to have a baby either, but I don't know…"

I move my arm forward like *go on.*

"The idea of this baby, this tiny human that was half me… Monica was talking about terminating the pregnancy. She wasn't ready. I wasn't ready. And she knew how important my baseball career was. I mean, everyone did. I was going to be drafted in the first round and offered millions of dollars. It should've been a no-brainer for both of us, but I just had this voice in my head, this feeling. I knew it would be hard being a young parent, but I asked Monica to keep the baby. She was shocked, and gave me the whole 'my body, my decision' speech, which was fine. I told her it wasn't about some political or spiritual belief. I just had a feeling. I told Monica if she would do this for me, if she would have the baby, I'd make sure she was taken care of until the child turned 18, even though she wouldn't have to be a part of the child's life. In fact, that was part of the deal. Monica wasn't allowed to see or come near the kid. When Jenny was born, Monica signed over her parental rights, and we made it all legal. I ended my baseball dreams to be a single father. No matter how good you are, you always spend a few years in the minor leagues, and travel around by bus and plane. There was no way I would put an infant through that. I changed course and went into law. Those years were hard but rewarding. My family helped out a lot while I made it through law school."

The whole thing sounded so crazy. I couldn't imagine basically selling my child off for an annuity, which is what it sounded like. "So, she just gave you Jenny? In exchange for a monthly paycheck?"

"I promised to help her financially if she stayed out of the way. She agreed."

"Wow." I'm speechless. I never really considered

having a family, but I could never just walk away from my child. I'm not really in a position to judge. I've never been through anything like that. If both parties were upfront and honest about their needs and wants, it almost sounded like a healthy transaction.

"Yeah." He rubs his jaw. "I wouldn't change my decision for anything in the world. That girl is my life." Decker fidgets with his cup for a second, then sets it down. His smoldering stare lands on me. "Look, I like you, Tate. I want to see where this goes, but at the same time, Jenny is the most important thing to me and will be until she's old enough to go out in the world as an adult."

I nod. "I understand. Honestly, I do. I think it's great you're so involved and take care of your child. Not many people would do what you did. Has dating been an issue for you in the past? I mean with Jenny."

"Nope." He answers the question immediately, without a hint of any doubt.

"Really? Never?"

Decker pauses for a moment, seemingly thinking through what he's about to say next. "I have a confession."

"Okay. Let's have it."

"You're the only woman I've dated that has ever met Jenny. Or been in our home, for that matter."

My heart skips a beat. My eyes feel like they might bug out of my head. Jenny is what, fourteen? And he's never dated another woman or brought her in the house to meet Jenny?

I don't think it's possible for Decker to look more serious than he does now. "I'm extremely guarded and protective when it comes to my daughter. Monica has never met her. I still get attention in the media because of what I do, and because of my past with baseball. I want Jenny to grow up as normal as possible, and I don't want another woman coming in here, getting to know her, then walking out and breaking her heart. You're the first, and to be quite honest, it scares me."

At his confession, I move from my chair and step over him to straddle his lap. My arms cradle his neck and our mouths fuse together.

He pulls me back for a second, his eyes still on mine. "This merger has to happen. It has to work, Tate, I'm serious."

"It will," I whisper, as I kiss along his neck.

He pulls me back away from him, so that we're eye to eye. "No, you don't understand. I have four years left with my daughter before she goes to college. If the merger happens, I'll be able to leave the office at five every day. I'll be able to make her dinner, go to her school functions, be a normal father. If it falls through, I'll be cleaning up the mess forever, and we have new clients that keep signing on, so many we can't keep up with them. I'm already working seventy-hour weeks. This merger is my ticket to a normal life with her. I'll never get these years back."

I put a hand out on his cheek. I don't know if it's too intimate already, but it just feels like the right thing to do. His love for his daughter reminds me of my own dad. The two of them are so different and yet so alike. My dad taught me to shoot guns, and fish, and ride horses, but the universal fatherly sentiment is the same. I remember how special that bond was for me, and I want him to have that with Jenny. It's priceless. "Decker, the merger will happen. We'll both see to it. Nobody can screw it up but us."

"That's what scares me."

I know he's baring his soul to me right now when he doesn't have to. The stakes are at an all-time high for him, and he's still pursuing me. "We won't mess it up. We can't."

Decker holds me close to him and then kisses me so hard it makes me dizzy. I pull back a little, gazing deeply into his eyes, wondering if this is all real or if he's too good to be true. He's smart, successful, talented… and he brought me to his house to cook for me and meet his daughter.

I regard him for a moment and quirk up an eyebrow. "You don't have any other secrets, do you?"

"I have a third nipple." He smirks.

I smack him playfully on the chest and laugh.

"No. I don't." He squeezes my butt and I rock against him, grinding over his erection that popped up during our kiss.

"I've seen your kitchen and eaten your food." I

gesture with my head back toward the house. “Now would be a good time to show me your bedroom.”

Decker grips my ass with both hands and stands up, carrying me in the process. His eyes turn dark and mischievous. “Oh, I have plenty more to show you.”

DECKER

WITH TATE'S legs around my waist and her arms around my neck, I carry her through the back door and down the hall to my bedroom. I'm not worried about Jenny. She's upstairs and sleeps with her TV on. We're downstairs at the opposite end of the house. The only thing on my mind is getting Tate naked, tasting every inch of her, and making her come so many times she passes out.

When we reach my bedroom, she slides down my body and lands on her feet. The complicated straps of her black dress won't deter me from taking what I want. I've been craving her the entire fucking week leading up to this dinner.

It's the edge of twilight and the glow of the moon shines through the blinds. I turn on my playlist and set it to low volume on shuffle. Tate takes a seat on the edge of my bed with a devilish grin, undoing the straps of her shoes. Tonight, I want her completely bare, nothing separating us. No clothes, nothing. I want her naked and panting, begging me to stop, to give her a second of reprieve before she has orgasm after orgasm. Her shoes drop to the hardwood floor and her lashes flutter as she watches me like a cat getting ready to play with its favorite toy.

I smirk at her. She might be used to being the predator but, right now, Tate Reynolds is my prey. I'm going to devour every inch of her until she's begging to submit. I'm the king and this is my castle.

Lifting my shirt over the back of my head, I toss it across the room, and it hits the floor. I reach for my belt, but Tate stops me. "Let me." Her red painted fingernails skim along my chest, tracing the contours of my muscles.

Her lips press to my stomach and she moves to undo my belt buckle. My fingers caress her jaw, moving down her neck to the straps of her dress that criss-cross over her chest and back.

"There's a zipper." She pops the button on my slacks, unzipping them, and shoving them down my thighs. My cock is rock-hard and tents my boxer briefs.

Tate runs a finger along my shaft, through the material, and I have to suck in a deep breath and stare up at the ceiling for a moment to collect my thoughts.

I step out of my pants and make good on getting her out of that damn dress. Once it's unzipped, I shimmy it down her ass and thighs and toss it over my head. She laughs as our lips meet and we fall back onto the mattress together. Tonight, I'm taking my time getting personal with every square inch of her. I'm going to worship her like the goddess she is.

Full of fevered kisses and with eager fingers, we collide. Her body melts into mine, molding into me like the missing piece of a puzzle. I kiss her soft and slow, tasting coffee and chocolate on her lips and smelling cinnamon in her hair. She's paradise, a little of heaven and hell. Tate is everything I could want in a woman. I've waited a lifetime to meet someone like her. Now, she's in my bed, mine for the taking. From the moment we first met, this is everything I've wanted.

I'll claim her body and her heart. After tonight, she'll be mine, and anyone who says differently is my enemy.

Her tongue sweeps along my lips and then thrusts inside my mouth. I slide her bra straps down her arms and jerk the lace cups to her stomach, exposing her rose-colored nipples. They're already hard and erect as I trace one of them with my index finger. She shudders at the sensation.

Good.

Her breasts are the perfect size, just enough to fill both hands. I kiss my way down her neck leaving a trail of teeth marks and hickeys low enough on her chest that she'll be able to cover them up at the office. Taking one of her nipples into my mouth, I suck hard then bite down on it while rolling the other between the pads of my thumb and forefinger. I keep repeating the motion, loving the way she gives me full control, opening herself completely to me. A soft purr escapes her lips, signaling her approval. I take her nipple between my front teeth, watching her face to log every reaction of what she likes and what she doesn't. I switch to her other breast and repeat my actions while sliding my free hand between her thighs.

Fuck, she's so wet it drips between her legs.

I take my time kissing my way down her torso, tasting every inch of her skin while my hands stay locked on both her breasts. Her chest rises and falls with labored breaths, each time pressing her tits harder against the grips I have on them.

I look up at her. Those honey-brown eyes lock onto mine.

"These fucking things are in my way." I growl the words and bite at the waistline of her lace thong. Her legs clench together around my face at the sudden intrusion of my head between her thighs. I take both of my hands, place them next to her pussy, and shove her knees apart forcefully.

She moans above me, her legs trying to squeeze back together but unable to break my hold. She gasps out a breath, but manages to say, "Take them off then, fuck." She draws out the last syllable, like she's not totally in control of her body but approves.

I tease at her sweet center with my mouth, kissing over her panties, then run my tongue the length of her pussy, back to front. Burying my face between her tan thighs, I can smell her arousal and my cock aches to be inside her.

Using my teeth, I yank half her thong down one of her legs, then repeat the motion on the other side. My plan is to pull them the rest of the way down with my hands to get them out of the way, but once I spot her glistening, pink cunt I'm like a feral animal.

I dive down onto it with my mouth, spreading her legs once more with my hands on her inner thighs. Her panties go taut and make a ripping sound.

"Jesus, Decker." She pants as she says the words. She doesn't say them like she's upset, more like she's going to come all over my face if I keep this up much longer.

Tate's pussy is sweet like honey and vanilla. I slide my tongue in lazy circles around her clit, then bite the tender part of her inner thigh hard enough to leave a bruise.

Her hands shoot into my hair and her nails dig into my scalp. The insides of her arms squeeze her tits together and, for a second, I think I might blow my load all over the bedsheets. It takes me a second to recover.

Her taut thong is still an obstacle I need out of my way if I'm going to eat her properly. I hook my fingers along the thin straps wrapped tightly around her thighs and tug them down her legs and off her feet.

I pause above her for a moment, her slick folds glistening beneath me, begging for my mouth and my cock. I look her straight in the eyes and say, "When you're getting dressed tomorrow, look at the mark I'm about to leave right here." I trace a finger on the soft flesh of her thigh. "Let it remind you who this pussy belongs to."

"Holy fu—"

She can't even finish her sentence before my mouth is on her. I slide my tongue in a large circle around the tender skin before biting down. Her entire body squirms and she lets out a yelp that carries through the room. Once I'm done, I drop kisses on the area over and over as my index finger circles her clit. Before long, she's bucking her hips at my face, trying to force my mouth back to her.

I put each of my hands behind both of her knees and shove her legs up toward her shoulders, bringing her pussy angled up to my mouth so I can dive straight down on top of it.

"Hold your legs here."

She hooks her arms around her legs, immediately following my order without thinking about it. Good. That's how I want her to react to my commands.

I dip my head down and suckle her clit between my lips, rolling, nibbling, swirling my tongue around it. I have this ability with Tate to be able to sense everything she's feeling. It's like a vibration running through her body that's on a frequency I'm in tune with.

As I continue to tongue her clit, I slide two fingers

in and out of her, then curl the tips up to meet the secret spot deep inside that drives her wild.

"I'm about to come, Decker."

At her admission, I slide my thumb into her pussy, just enough to get it wet, then drag it down and press it against her tight little asshole.

She squirms again and her whole body goes tense. She starts to let go of her legs, and I shove them back up against her shoulders with my free hand. "I said hold your legs, Tate."

"So close."

I give her ass a quick smack, trying to introduce a little pleasureful pain to keep her orgasm at bay. It doesn't seem to do much to help. She's coiled up like a spring, like a pressure cooker about to blow its top.

I continue to swirl my thumb against her puckered asshole while I tongue her clit, each moment increasing the intensity, slowly building. Right when I think she can't take it anymore, I look up at her. She's staring back, her eyes straining to focus on me. I give her a nod, and she lets loose right as I bury my entire face in her pussy.

Her toes curl and her feet plant themselves next to me on the bed. Her hips rise and buck as the orgasm rips through her body. I keep my mouth latched onto her the entire time, not giving her one second of reprieve. Her whole body trembles and quivers as her hands fist the sheets into small bunches of Egyptian cotton. She's so fucking hot, and watching her come turns on the animalistic instincts from the ancient part of my brain, where humans were only made to procreate to help the species survive. Evolution turned us into civilized creatures, but one look at Tate right now, and my hips start rutting into the sheets. It's uncontrollable, the urge to fuck her, come inside her, mark her as mine. I keep fucking the covers on the bed as my mouth devours her pussy right as her orgasm crests.

"Fuck, Decker."

I love the way my name rolls off her tongue as she draws it out.

Finally, after a few seconds, she relaxes, her whole body still quaking with post-orgasm ecstasy. I finally regain control of myself and continue to run my tongue up and down her slit as she tries to push my mouth away from her body. She breathes heavily, unable to lift her head from the bed. I work my way back up toward her face, trailing kisses in my wake. I slide my tongue across one of her nipples and she shudders, goosebumps pebbling across her skin.

I smile once I work my way up to her mouth.

"Enjoy that?"

She shakes her head, still panting. "You're so fucking—"

"Good, amazing, incredible?"

She grips the back of my neck like she's pulling me in for a kiss but stops me in front of her face. "Cocky or arrogant would have been my choice of words."

Before I can respond, her mouth crashes into mine.

My cock is rock-hard now and pressed up against her entrance, halfway parting her lips. I want nothing more than to shove into her and fuck her so hard she can't walk for a week. But not yet.

I want to take her to the edge of the cliff of another orgasm with nothing but my tongue and fingers and pull her back over and over again until she begs me to let her come again. This is all about pleasing her. Showing her that her needs are important to me… that *she* is important to me.

I work my way back down, so that my mouth is inches from her pussy, and she gives me a look like she can't handle anymore right now. Sliding my fingers through her heat, I watch her reaction, loving the way her mouth parts to let out the most erotic whimpers. I keep doing it, over and over.

"You're making me crazy," she whines, arching her hips up and threading her fingers in my hair. "That tongue has magical powers." After taking a break for a few seconds, she gives me a playful yank and I suck on her clit again. Her body pulses with desire. It doesn't take long before she's coming on my mouth once more. Nothing but frantic hands and deep breaths, before she arches her hips up in the air and says my name over and over.

My cock is so goddamn hard I think I might pass out, and I can't hold back any longer. I need to be inside her. I kiss my way back up her body until our mouths meet and she guides me in. It takes everything I have to hold back and not fuck her so hard my thighs bruise her ass. I want this to be special and intimate, not like the quickie in the office.

I want to take my time and be in the moment, the two of us joined together. As my cock slides in, my eyes roll back in my head at her wet heat squeezing around me. There's something about being inside Tate Reynolds. It just feels like I'm—home. Like everything is right in the world, just how it's supposed to be. I look into her eyes and brush her hair back from her face. "You're perfect, Tate."

"Mmm." She moans into my mouth, arching her back while unable to form words. Our bodies move in tandem in a delicious game of push and pull. Her walls tighten around me as I slide in and out, slow and steady. Gradually, I go deeper with each gentle thrust.

Her body ripples with pleasure and she cries out. I grin at her and roll to my back.

"I want you on top, grinding that pussy on my dick." I slap her ass as she straddles my thighs and I watch as she puts my cock inside her and slowly sinks down on it.

"Fuck," I groan.

Tate rolls her hips, moving from side to side, riding me at a languid pace. She leans down and slides her breasts up my chest so she can kiss me. I grip the back of her hair, and wrap another hand around her waist, just above her ass, then push her down on me as I thrust up.

She moans her approval in my ear, over and over as she rocks back and forth on me.

She finally leans back and straightens so that she's upright. Her hips begin to grind. "Oh my God, Decker." Her body starts to quiver.

I take my thumb and rub circles around her clit as she rocks harder and faster.

"Just like that, Tate. I want to watch you come on my cock."

And I do just that. Within a few seconds she's trembling, and I feel her pussy tighten around me. I'm not sure how much longer I'll be able to last before I blow, but it doesn't matter. I have all night long to do whatever I want to her.

I thrust up in long, hard, sweet strokes, loving the feel of her. Tate crashes forward and I capture her mouth. Her nails dig into my shoulders as she rides out her release.

Once she's done, her head collapses onto my neck and her mouth is next to my ear. "It's your turn to come."

"Don't worry, it's gonna happen any second." I slide up into her hot pussy once more, taking her as deep as possible.

"I bet I can make it happen faster."

"You wish you had that kind of control over me." I smirk, playing her little game. It's quite fun, but she knows who's in charge.

"I'll make you come in five seconds or less, Decker Collins."

I laugh for a quick second, though it's difficult when Tate's hot pussy keeps gliding up and down my dick, and the whole goal is to not come when she wants me to.

"I'll take that bet."

She nods. "Okay, you ready?"

"Whenever you are. Just say when." I immediately start thinking about anything I can that might take my mind off blowing inside her in the next five seconds.

Tate leans down in my ear. "I know what you really want, Decker. What you need to get off."

"And what's that?"

"I want you to fuck me like a dirty little whore and blow deep inside my pussy."

Before I know what's happened, an orgasm rushes to the head of my cock. Tate starts bouncing up and down as hard as she can, right on my cock, her fingers digging into my scalp.

I get two thrusts in, her ass clapping on my thighs, before every muscle in my body constricts and my balls lift high and tight. About three seconds have passed and there's no way I can hold out any longer. My cock kicks deep inside her and hot jets of come shoot into the depths of her pussy.

Once she finishes riding out my orgasm, she presses her forehead against mine. "Told you."

I shake my head at her. "You cheated."

She laughs. "I can't help it if I know what you want. It's the same way you know what I need. We're just like this." She holds up her hand and twists her index and middle finger together. "Can't explain it." She shrugs. "Oh, and Decker?"

"Yeah?"

"Told you I always win." She winks.

I can't help but smile. I brush a few sweaty strands of hair from her cheeks. Her sated eyes meet mine. I stare at her, a hundred percent serious. "I really like you." I can't say I love her, obviously, but fuck me if it doesn't feel that way. I don't know how or why. All I know is, I've never felt this way about another woman, and I want her to know I'm serious. She gets what I'm hinting at judging by the reaction on her face.

"What?" She fights a smile and her cheeks turn a slight shade of pink. Rolling away from me she lets out a breath and looks back over. "You're caught up in the moment."

"I wouldn't have brought you here if I didn't *like* you. I know what I'm saying, what I feel." Sweaty and breathless, I slide closer and pull her into me. Her head falls to my chest. My heartbeat races as she looks at me. But her stare is different. It's like she's looking inside me and can see all my good qualities and all my faults. She looks at me like she knows what I feel, and she feels it too.

"We're doomed, aren't we?"

"Why do you say that?" I let out a light laugh and trace the outline of a circle on her shoulder.

Tate moves up on her elbow and props her chin up on her hand. "Because, I like you too."

I lean over and kiss her, wanting to be inside her again after hearing the words roll off her tongue.

"Where do we go from here? Do you have to go back to Dallas? When the merger is complete?"

Tate's eyes dart to the ceiling, like she's contemplating her answer. "I don't know. I love it here in Chicago. Not just because you're here. It's a beautiful city. I have my family to think about back home, though. My brothers and my nephews."

"You can always go see them or bring them here to visit."

"True." She curls back into me. "I don't know what Weston has planned for me when this is through. We've been laser focused on making it happen. I'm sure we'll figure it out once it's done."

Her ass presses against my cock. Sliding my hand past the curve of her hip down between her thighs, I stroke her clit.

As her legs part, she looks right at me. "Last time started slow and intimate. I really enjoyed it."

"But?" I grin.

"It's time to fuck me the way you want, Decker."

"Might regret that." My eyes narrow.

I only say it to see how she'll react, and she doesn't

disappoint. Her pulse speeds up on her neck and she looks—nervous.

Good.

My fingers dig into her hips and I flip her onto her stomach, hard. She lets out a light squeal and I smack her on the ass, hard enough to leave a pink handprint. I run my finger over it lightly, relishing the mark.

Right when she's about to make a smartass remark, I grip the sides of her hips and yank her ass up to my cock. I fist my shaft in my right hand, and use my left to shove her chest down to the mattress.

"Only your ass in the air, sweetheart."

"So demanding."

I reach down and grip a handful of hair, angling her face up toward the ceiling, but keeping her back arched so her chest still presses into the mattress. I line up my cock and slam into her from behind. There's no soft and sweet, this is about showing her who's in charge in the bedroom. I slide my fingers from her hair around to the slender column of her throat as I hammer into her from behind, driving my cock hard and fast. She gasps for air. My thighs smack into her ass so hard the clapping sounds echo through the room.

She tries to say something, but her words vibrate and come out in a jumbled mess that ends in her moaning over and over. Her body trembles, and I know she's about to come again. I have the exact same problem. My balls tighten and swell. I stare down at her small, hourglass figure, and she slams back into me as I thrust into her.

"That's it. Fuck that dick like a dirty little slut."

"Holy shit, Decker." Her words come out on a pant.

Her body quakes, her orgasm coming on quick. She squeezes around me, and I can't take it any longer. Her tight, wet pussy grips down on me and sends me over the edge. I shove her down flat on the bed, pinning her with my hips and chest, and I shove as deep into her as humanly possible. I let loose and come inside her once more as she rides out her orgasm.

We remain joined until her breathing evens out, and I kiss down her neck, shoulders, and back.

"Decker?"

"Yeah?"

"I hate to ruin the mood, but I have to tell you something. You're not gonna like it." Her eyes are half-hooded like she's about to pass out.

"Is it about us?" I sit up, a jolt of fear slamming into my chest.

"It's work."

I breathe a sigh of relief as she goes on to tell me about Donavan's lawsuit against her client.

Fucking Donavan.

I need to go through and review everything in the documents, but I already know it's him trying to tank the merger.

"Don't worry about it right now. I'll take care of it." I pepper kisses all over her, until she falls asleep. I slip out of bed and turn the fan on. It's hot in the room and I want her to be comfortable. I want Tate to know I cherish her, and I'll do whatever it takes to take care of her.

I watch her sleep, hoping like hell when all is said and done, I get to keep her. I want her to be mine. I don't want her going back to Dallas, and I'll fight Weston and my brothers if I have to. I don't want her anywhere else, but with me.

Not now.

Not ever.

I want Tate Reynolds for the rest of my life.

TATE

My body aches as I stretch. I wake up in Decker's king-sized bed, but the other side is empty. My clothing is folded and lying on a chair. There's a note on the pillow.

Tate,

Last night was perfect. I'm in the kitchen. Put these on and join me for breakfast.

Decker

There's a pair of plaid pajama bottoms and a V-neck white tee laid out for me. They're both my size.

Did he go buy pajamas while I was asleep?

I help myself to a shower. His private bath is immaculate. On one side is a clawfoot tub with an adjacent open-door shower with so many heads I don't know if I can figure out how to work the freaking thing. I find towels in his walk-in closet attached to the bathroom. I'm sure Jenny has some girlie shampoo and soap upstairs but I'm not about to ask. I pick up the black bottle and take a whiff. It smells like Decker. I'm not washing my hair here though. I snag a scrunchie from my clutch and sweep my hair up to keep it from getting wet.

I look down as the water cascades over my body and see the bite marks on the insides of my thighs. I think back to what Decker said and a wave of tingling courses through my body.

"When you're getting dressed tomorrow, look at the mark I'm about to leave right here. Let it remind you who this pussy belongs to."

Fuck, he's so damn possessive and just, hot.

After my shower, I slip on the pajamas and walk through the house.

The smell of bacon wafts down the hallway and my stomach growls. Decker worked my body out good last night. I'm a little sore, but in the best way possible. I walk into the kitchen to find him cooking breakfast. He's wearing that goofy apron again. Jenny sits at the breakfast bar with a book, eating a bowl of fruit and yogurt.

"Morning." Jenny smiles at me.

My cheeks must turn some shade of pink. I hope she's okay with me staying over, but I guess it's a little too late for her to complain. She doesn't seem to mind one bit, though, judging by her reactions. She seems genuinely happy her father is happy.

"Hope you're hungry. Dad's cooking enough to feed the neighborhood."

Decker sticks his tongue out at her. He walks over to me with a mixing bowl, stirring pancake batter. His lips meet mine and I pull back to smirk at him. "Show off." I glance at the spread taking up half the counter space. Sitting in front of us are eggs, bacon, fruit, yogurt, sausage, and now the man is making pancakes.

"I wasn't sure what you'd prefer. So, I made a little bit of everything. It's overkill I know." I swear he looks embarrassed by his actions and it's adorable.

"It's sweet. Thank you. I don't eat a heavy breakfast, though." I grab a piece of bacon and help myself to one of the mugs of coffee.

"Told you, Dad."

I listen to the two of them bicker and, oddly, I don't feel out of place. I'm enjoying myself and get the impression Jenny likes having me here too.

I continue sipping my coffee and crunch a piece of bacon between my teeth. It's not lost on me that Decker cooks bacon the appropriate way, crispy.

The two of them go out of their way to make me feel welcome and keep asking me if I need anything else. After the third "no" they take the hint I'm content watching the two of them in their element. Decker finishes making the pancakes and fills his plate when the doorbell rings.

"I'll get it. It's probably, Joselyn." Jenny pushes off from the counter.

"Her *bestie*." Decker sits down on a barstool.

"Bestie, huh?" I laugh at his attempt at teenage vernacular.

"Yep. They're Gucci."

"Okay, just stop, Decker." I put a hand on his forearm.

He grins. God, the first day I walked into his office, I never thought I'd hear him cracking dad jokes. This is all surreal.

"Dad, there's some lady at the door."

Decker groans and drops his fork. When he gets up, he freezes. His hackles rise and his face turns fiery red.

I glance back to see what pissed him off. I've only seen him look this mad once before, and it was at his office.

Sure enough, it's the same reason today. Jenny walks into the kitchen with Monica, and I can see the whole story written on the poor girl's face. She knows Monica's her mother.

I should worry about how Jenny processes the moment, but all I can think about is how this woman ruins every single great moment between Decker and me.

"What the hell, Monica?" Decker's tone is low but deadly.

"I tried calling, but you never answered. Guess I see why. Too busy playing house."

I know it's not my place to get involved but Jenny is on the verge of tears and Decker is about to pop a blood vessel. I feel protective of them even though our relationship—or whatever this is—is still new. "Get out." The words tumble from my mouth before I think them through.

"What?" Monica glares at me and looks to Decker.

"Don't look at him. Look at me." I don't know what I'm doing, but I can't stop speaking. "You shouldn't be here. When Decker is ready to talk, he'll call you." I move toward her and she takes a step back.

"You don't tell me what to do."

"You need to leave. Now."

Jenny rushes to her dad and he wraps her in a hug. He moves her out the back door onto the deck. I'm not sure how he'll feel about me butting in, but this woman is ridiculous.

"He owes me." Monica's bottom lip quivers.

"He owes you?" I laugh. "Decker owes you nothing. If anything, you should be grateful he raised your daughter and doesn't sue your ass for child support. He's a lot nicer than I am, lady. I'm sure he'll get your money for you. He always keeps his word. But you bother him or upset Jenny again, you'll deal with me. Are we clear?"

"Crystal," she murmurs. "Tell him I'll be waiting out front."

I nod and she spins around on her heels and flips her hair, leaving me alone in the kitchen. The backdoor opens and Jenny bolts up the back staircase to her bedroom.

Decker stares at me and, for the first time, I can't read how he's feeling.

"Umm… Monica's waiting out front for you to write her a check."

He nods.

"Is Jenny okay?"

"She'll be fine. She's always known about Monica." He sighs. "Just never met her."

"Sorry I butted in. Figured it'd give you a chance to get Jenny away. I just felt protective of you guys."

"Thank you. I appreciate the sentiment."

I can't tell if he's mad, happy, or just indifferent. He's keeping his cool way better than I would've thought he could. Maybe it's the fact Jenny is here. I admire his restraint at the moment. He's stoic—fatherly. I guess that's what being a good parent means. Not losing your shit in front of your kids, no matter how bad you want to. "If you want me to go, I get it. I know it's not my place."

Decker steps in close. "I care about you, Tate, and I love that you stuck up for Jenny and me." He leans down and gives me a quick kiss.

"Shouldn't you go out there?"

"Let her squirm." He kisses me harder. A few minutes pass and he eventually pulls away to deal with Monica.

DECKER

I CAN'T BELIEVE Monica had the nerve to come here knowing Jenny would probably be home. I walk into the living room and peek out the blinds. She's waiting in the doorway. She has on tight jeans and a purple top cut way too low, showing off the boob job I'm positive I paid for. If not me, some other unsuspecting sap footed the bill. I wonder if the poor bastard she's met has any freaking clue what he signed up for with this piece of work. Looking back, I can't believe I fell into bed with her, but when you're young you do stupid shit.

The worst part is, I know Monica's a good person. I think it's the way she was raised. From what I could gather her parents were both this way. Always looking for a handout, never working for anything. It's hard to assign blame to someone for the way they are, when it's all they've ever known.

There's a black sedan parked on the street with

tinted windows. I can't tell if anyone else is in it or not. Monica stares at the front door waiting for me to come out. I need a few minutes to get my temper in control. If I walk out there now who knows what I'll say to her. I don't want to yell loud enough for Jenny to hear. On top of everything, regardless of what Monica does, she's still Jenny's biological mother. My daughter is part her.

I'm glad Tate stepped in so I could get Jenny away from the situation as soon as possible. I know I'm being overprotective; Jenny is fourteen. She's a young woman now, but I don't see myself ever not shielding her from dangerous people. Dangerous in the sense they could harm her emotionally as well as physically. I tried playing it nice in my office when she showed up. It's time to take the gloves off. This shit has to end. We had an arrangement, and Monica broke it coming here.

I honestly thought Jenny would be more upset. All she said to me was, "Is that my mother?" I could've lied to her, but I didn't. We don't lie to each other. I don't keep anything from her, and I won't start now.

Jenny was upset, but she's a tough kid with a good head on her shoulders. She's always known her mother wouldn't be in the picture. I took her to therapy when she was little to make sure it didn't cause any abandonment issues. I rake a hand through my hair and go into my office to grab my checkbook.

Monica doesn't deserve a dime for pulling this shit, but I want her gone from our lives for good. I won't have her setting Jenny back or hurting her more than she already has. Taking a deep breath, I open the door. Monica wipes at her eyes but I don't give a damn if she was crying. I did my best to stay on good terms with her—paid her a ton of money, and this is how she repays me.

I keep my voice down to a whisper, but by the end it's almost a whisper-scream. "What the fuck were you thinking, showing up? At. My. God. Damn. House. We had an arrangement."

"Sorry, Decker, I just started thinking after our talk the other day. I saw that picture in your office and wondered if she thinks about me or asks about me. You know? It was stupid, I know that now. It's just I'm her mom and we've never met. She's beautiful, though, and so polite. I didn't mean to upset her, I swear."

"How selfish can you be? Did you even ask yourself what showing up here might do to her? And for fuck's sake, she's a child. Of course she wondered about you, when she was five years old, but not now. She knows you'll never be part of her life. That was the agreement. You don't get to say*, oh oopsie it's been fourteen years but guess what, I'm your mom*. I know you and, in a month, or hell a week, you'll be with the next man and Jenny will be a fading memory. I'm not having it."

"She probably thinks I'm a monster anyway."

"Don't." I shake my head and point my finger. "Don't pull that shit. Not right now. I'm too upset."

"What shit?"

"That psychological manipulation, where you say

things like that. Assume I've painted you in an unflattering way, and that's why she wants nothing to do with you. It's not true. Fact is, we don't talk about you much. But we used to. And I have never uttered one bad thing about you to that girl in there. As a matter of fact, I embellished on the good side. I don't want her thinking her mother is a bad person. Why would I do that? She's half you, you get that, right?"

Monica stares at me with surprise in her eyes. Like she thought this whole time I've told Jenny she's the devil.

I sigh. "Look, you can't be here."

"I understand. I wasn't thinking."

"You never are, are you?"

"That woman seems to care about you guys a lot. It's the same one from your office, isn't it?"

"That's none of your concern." I open the checkbook, but she keeps on.

"I may not be mother of the year, but I still care about you and Jenny."

I snort. Monica's only out for number one. "I guess we're moving on to manipulation tactic number two, where you pretend you care about us now. Look, you're the woman who gave birth to Jenny. Nothing more. So, don't come here acting all righteous like you've ever given a damn about her or me."

"That's not true." She frowns.

"We're done here. Tell me how much so I can sign this check. And once I do, this is it. It's the last one, so make it count. I don't want to see you. I don't want to hear from you. I don't want you to think about Jenny or me again. We're dead to you." I was fine giving her money when she kept away but this stunt today sent me over the edge.

"That's it? You're just buying me off?"

"That was the deal fourteen years ago. I'm just expediting it to a lump sum payout. Give me a number."

She looks at her feet and mumbles, "Fifty."

My jaw ticks but I prop the checkbook on the front door. I fill out the check and rip it from the book. "I give you this money and you promise we're done, or I'll let Tate have a go at you. She's one of the top attorneys in the country and she'd love nothing more than to haul your ass into a courtroom. You don't want to be on the other end of that."

"I promise. I told you I'm leaving Chicago."

"Good."

Monica takes the check and starts for the end of the driveway, then turns back. A tear slides down her cheek. "I'm not a monster, am I?"

I shake my head. There's nothing I'd like more than to shake the shit out of her, but I just can't be cruel. Not too harsh, anyway. I don't know if it's because of our past, or because I see a little bit of Jenny in her. "You're not a monster, Monica. You're just—" I shake my head, searching for the words. "You didn't have the best examples growing up. I'm not blaming your parents for who you are, but it makes a difference. There are a lot of good things about you. I really do wish you the best, and hope you find whatever makes you happy. It just can't be our daughter."

Monica nods. "You really are a great father, and you've been good to me over the years. Can't say the same for myself. I'm sorry."

I walk out to her, because I don't want her to think I hate her. I just want her gone. Once I'm in front of her, I put a hand on her shoulder. "I forgive you, okay?"

She nods and tears stream down her face, even more this time.

"If you show up in Jenny's life without permission again, there will be serious problems. Maybe when she's an adult she'll contact you. That's up to her."

"Okay."

I turn toward the door. "Good luck, Monica."

I walk to the porch and never look back.

TATE

I GO UPSTAIRS and seek out Jenny. She's in the TV room lying on a dark brown leather sectional flipping through the movie channels. I knock gently on the door. "Can I come in?"

She shrugs her shoulders.

I enter and smile when she selects Twilight.

"Team Edward or team Jacob?"

"You like Twilight?" She seems skeptical.

I collapse into the armchair. "Totally. I read the books two times."

"No way."

"Way!"

She laughs.

"I started out team Jacob because I accidentally read New Moon first, but the second time I came around to team Edward."

"I'm team Rosalie."

I freeze. "What?"

"Bella should have chosen herself. She had these two guys who were both right and wrong for her for different reasons, but she should've kicked them to the curb and gone for that nice guy, Mike."

"Smart girl." I know she'll eventually appreciate the brooding bad boys like the rest of us, as long as they turn into redeeming nice guys once their layers are peeled back. Sort of like someone I think about at that exact moment.

We get about ten minutes into the movie when Decker joins us. "There you are."

He comes into the room and grabs my hand. "Come with me."

"No way. Jenny and I are watching a movie. You're welcome to join us."

Decker snorts. "Sorry, I don't do sparkling vampires and teenage angst. Come find me after."

"I will."

He kisses my cheek and Jenny smiles at us.

"If you're not busy, we could use some snacks." I grin.

Jenny nods. "I'm thirsty too."

"How about a pizza?"

"Only if it's homemade," says Jenny.

"I'll need to run to the store for that."

Jenny looks at me then pauses the movie. "If Tate's cool with it can we all go and when we get back, she can help us in the kitchen? You can even pick the movie so we can all watch something together."

A warm tingling rushes through my body. She wants to spend time with me and wants to include me in her time with her dad. I wasn't sure what to expect when Decker said he wanted to see where things go with us. Things are moving pretty fast in a hurry. I know his daughter is his world, but it means so damn much to me that they're trying to make me part of theirs.

I look at Decker and he gives me a smile.

I shrug. "Okay. Let's do it."

The three of us load up in the car and Jenny rides in back even though I offered to.

Decker places a hand on my thigh and gives me a gentle squeeze before we get out.

Jenny pushes the shopping cart and Decker and I follow behind holding hands. I can't help but feel sentimental and a little nostalgic. I remember growing up, most of my friends' moms always did their shopping alone, but not mine. She loved it when my dad went to the store with her, even if he did frown most of the way through the trip. They did everything together, the classic old couple with the serious, grumpy husband who every once in a while cracks a dry joke that has everyone rolling. It makes me miss home a little.

If I moved to Chicago, I'd be leaving all my family behind. I can't recall anyone, even in my extended family, living outside of Texas.

"Okay. Toppings." Jenny grabs sauce, pepperoni, peppers, ham, and lastly pineapple.

My nose scrunches up and my mouth screws into a disgusted pout.

"You don't like pineapple on pizza?" Jenny's green eyes widen.

"Not a fan, sorry."

"That's okay, we can make two. One for me and one for you guys. Dad doesn't like it either, but I usually make him eat it anyway."

I was afraid it would be a strike against me. Monica has no idea what she missed out on with Jenny and Decker. That's okay, though, it left the door open for me to come into their lives.

BACK AT THE HOUSE, Decker wears his ridiculous apron, but it looks so freaking hot on him. No other man could pull off a blue apron with a mustache on it that says—I mustache you a question. Got beef?

I laugh to myself every time I look at the damn thing.

Jenny plays some bubblegum pop music and dances around us, sprinkling toppings over the sauce.

I can see myself wanting this to be my life, spending weekends with the two of them, goofing off, making memories.

Decker pops the pizzas in the oven and sets a timer.

"What are we watching, Dad?"

"Let Tate pick." He smirks at me and my stomach rolls.

"Way to put a girl on the spot, *sweetheart*." I tap my chin trying to think of something appropriate we'll all enjoy.

"No pressure." Jenny sticks her tongue out at me.

"Um. Have you guys watched the Jurassic Park movies?"

"Not the newest one. Remember, Jenny, you had that science fair project the weekend it came out? The one where you thought it was a good idea to make homemade slime, but it ended up stuck in your hair somehow."

"Oh yeah." She laughs. "That was a terrible idea."

While Jenny finds the movie on Amazon, I walk back to the kitchen to help Decker get the pizzas and grab some plates and drinks.

His arms wrap around my waist from behind as I set the plates on the counter and he kisses my neck. "I like this. Having you here with us. It's nice."

"I like it too." I twist around to face him.

Decker looks at me all sweet. "Jenny likes you. I was worried she wouldn't. Should've known better."

"Me too." I laugh and he kisses me again.

He lowers his voice to where Jenny can't hear. "This is all amazing, Tate. But if I'm being honest, it scares the hell out of me at the same time. Are you scared?"

"Decker…" I touch his face. "This is all new to me too. I've never dated anyone with a kid before."

"You're doing pretty damn amazing so far." He squeezes my butt, and I lean into him. Our mouths inch closer together and I part my lips in invitation for him to kiss me again.

"Is the pizza ready? Movie's about to start." Jenny's voice carries in from the other room.

We break apart and I clear my throat. "Be right there."

Decker winks at me. "We'll finish this later." He glances down to my ass and my breasts. It quickly reminds me he's still the dirty, hot man who put bite marks on my thighs and chest.

I lick my lips and heat flames to life in the pit of my stomach.

This man may very well be the one for me.

The thought terrifies and excites me at the same time.

I grab our drinks and take them to the TV room, placing the glasses on coasters.

"Were you two making out?" Jenny teases and my face goes bright pink. "Oh my God, you totally were." She giggles and I shake my head.

This kid is something else. I have to remind myself I was fourteen once.

DECKER

Tate struts into my office carrying a stack of files.

I arch my brows at her. "What the hell is that?"

"My excuse for coming to your office. Research for a really big case." She slams the files down on my desk and locks my door after turning down the blinds. "I'm afraid we'll have to work through lunch. If we want to finish it all." She starts toward me as I flick through the files full of blank paper. I start to laugh, but my laughter dies when her dress hits the floor.

I move to get up, but she wags a red manicured nail at me. "Nuh uh. Stay right where you are, Mr. Collins. I checked with your assistant, and she assured me you're free until one-thirty. For the next hour, your schedule's full of nothing but me."

She grabs hold of my tie and yanks me forward, thrusting her tongue between my lips. I go rock-hard as she straddles me in my chair. The woman has the art of seduction down that's for damn sure. I look right into her eyes, and give her my best cocky smirk. "You're about to be full of nothing but me."

"He sticks the landing like a pro."

"That layup isn't worthy of a response." The yellow pushup bra she wears corrals her tits. Her nipples show through the thin lace material. I rub one hand over her breasts and cup her tight ass with the other.

"What'd I do before you came into my life?" I growl, nipping at her lips.

"Play shitty golf." She rolls her hips, rubbing her hot pussy over my erection.

I grin. "Gonna get yourself in trouble."

"Mmm." She grinds on me. "That a promise? I could use some discipline."

"Fuck, I need inside you."

"Not yet. I'm in control. I set the meeting, remember?" Her lips curve upward into a mischievous smirk. She gets up from my lap and drops to her knees. "I want these off, Mr. Collins."

Fuck, I can't think of anything I want more than her lips wrapped around my cock, smearing that hooker-red lipstick up and down my shaft. "I like when you call me Mr. Collins. Makes me feel powerful."

"Good. Now shut the fuck up and let me suck your dick, Mr. Collins." She pushes my legs apart and undoes my belt. My cock springs free and Tate licks her red-stained lips. She slips off her bra and tosses it aside.

Wrapping a fist around my shaft, she jerks me right between her tits.

Fuck. I knew she was dirty, but this is taking it to a new level. It takes immeasurable restraint not to blow my load all over her chest.

Her mouth comes down on my cock and she licks the tip, swirling her tongue in a circular motion over the head and up and down the shaft. Tate's lips stretch wider accepting me into her mouth while she teases at my balls, rolling them with her fingers.

I thrust my hips and grab her hair, taking over. My restraint only goes so far. I fuck her sweet mouth, pushing farther with every stroke until I hit the back of her throat and she gags. Tears leak from the corners of her eyes, but Tate is no quitter and sucks me harder, flattening her tongue against me, taking every inch.

"You okay?"

She glares at me and takes me even farther into her mouth to prove a point. I love how competitive she is.

Just when I'm about to come, she slips me from her mouth and stands up. She winks then bends over my desk in her best Marilyn Monroe type pose and wiggles her ass at me. Pushing up out of the chair, my pants drop to my ankles and I stand behind her.

The fake files go sailing off the edge of the desk and I splay my fingers across her upper back and shove her down, pressing her tits against the hard wood. Her head lays to the side and she grips the edge for support.

Jerking her panties down her thighs and spreading

her legs wide, I slide a finger into her soaked pussy and bring it to my mouth for a pre-fuck taste. It only makes my cock harder in my palm. Without thinking, I fist a handful of her hair, and smack her once across the ass, just to see my handprint.

She lets out a whispered yelp of approval, then smiles back at me.

I cup her pussy from behind. "This is mine, *sweetheart*. You belong to me. Only me."

"God yes." She moans the words on a pant, beneath me as I line my cock up behind her.

I ease into her hot cunt and a shudder rips through me. Gripping her hips, I pump in and out of her tight center, delivering punishing strokes, bringing her close to the edge over and over again. Each time I stop just long enough to leave her hanging. With my free hand, I bend out to the side and wrap my arm under her waist so I can stroke her clit while I pound into her.

I thrust as hard as I can, and the desk moves an inch. The whole office might know we're fucking but right now I don't care. I know I'm falling hard.

Truth be told, I never thought I'd meet anyone who could make me want to commit, but Tate makes me want to try. She's worth it.

I pull out and slam back in. A bead of sweat trickles down her spine and she clenches around me. I lean back and watch myself hammering in and out of her. "Play with your pussy while I fuck you."

"Fuck, your filthy mouth does things to me,

Decker." Her hand goes straight to her clit and I feel her fingers brush against my balls every time I slam into her.

My cock glistens as she coats my dick with her juices, and it turns me on even more. After a few more deep strokes, I pull out and grunt, shooting my hot load across her. My orgasm seems to never stop as I stare at her ass and pump my cock with my hand, marking her skin with my release. With ownership.

She smiles back all breathless and sated.

The words I love you hang on the tip of my tongue but I'm afraid it's too soon to say them. So I hold them back, lean over, and place a kiss on her back.

"Let's get you cleaned up." I walk off to my bathroom, my cock still hanging half-mast between my legs. I grab some towels and return to clean her up. She's still bent over my desk showing off her come-covered ass. Sweat rolls down my back and I don't think I've ever been happier.

My cell phone rings with a call from my daughter.

"Is everything okay?" She never calls from school unless it is an emergency.

"It's fine. I was calling to ask if I can stay over at Joselyn's tonight. Her mom said she would take us to the mall and help us pick out dresses for the father daughter dance. But I wanted to ask you a question."

"Okay, go ahead."

"Do you, um, think Tate would be weirded out if I asked her to meet me at the mall?"

Wow, I don't know if I was ready for that. Things really are moving fast, and it's a reminder of how quick I've brought Tate into our lives. At the same time, it warms my heart that Jenny would think of Tate for something like this. "Umm no, slugger. I think she'd enjoy that."

"Cool. It's just that Mrs. Lykans doesn't have great taste and Tate's a good dresser. She has style."

I laugh. "You want to ask her, or you want me to do it?"

"I can call her, unless you think it'd be better if you did. I know you guys are just starting to get serious. I don't want to scare her off."

I smile at how thoughtful Jenny is. I raised this girl. "I'll text you the number. Tate likes you."

"I like her too. Love you, Dad."

"Love you too, slugger." I smile and text the number after ending the call.

Ten minutes later Tate storms into my office and paces back and forth. Her hair is still a little disheveled, but I don't point it out. "I take it Jenny called you?"

"Yup." She nods clasping her hands together.

"You okay with that? I never would've given her your number if I thought it would be weird for you."

"It's not that." She shakes her head. "I'm nervous. I don't want to mess up. What if she hates whatever I pick out? I'm not experienced in this. Can I buy her makeup and take her to get her nails done? I'll treat her friend too." She rambles on about taking Mrs. Lykans to dinner.

I grab her by the shoulders. "Breathe. It'll be fine."

She sucks in a breath. "Okay. I got this."

"You do."

DONAVAN MARCHES toward my office and he's seething. Thank God Deacon and Dexter at least seem to be on board with the merger. Two out of three is better than I expected, so I still chalk it up as a win.

He yanks the door open and stomps toward my desk. "You dropped my lawsuit? Talked to my client behind my back?"

"It was a loser and you know it."

"I have a responsibility to my client. If someone is stealing…"

I've heard enough. "Oh, shut the fuck up, Donavan." I march up and get right in his face. "I know you're not on board with this merger. I got the memo. But you know why I need it to happen. Think about your niece, at least. Your behavior is reckless."

He paces back and forth. "Your little girlfriend went running to you, didn't she? She knew I'd kick her ass in the courtroom and couldn't take the heat. These are the kind of people you want to work under."

"I won't be under anyone, and neither will you. You're acting like a petulant child. And for the record, Tate would've murdered you in court and you know it. I'm thinking about pulling all your cases, because this was the most irresponsible shit I've ever seen. Which is totally out of character for you. I'd expect something like this from the twins."

"I bet you didn't even review the files. You probably just jumped when she called and took her side immediately. You're fucking whipped."

I let out an exasperated sigh. "Look at me when I'm talking to you."

Donavan glances over.

"You think I'm taking sides? I read the files and reviewed everything before I went to your client, who happens to be my client too. Yeah, I saw your college buddy's name in the documents. The computer science guy you brought home once at Christmas. The guy was always a fucking asshole. You never even liked him. The case is a loser and we don't lose. So yeah, I went to our client and told them I didn't want to keep billing them for it."

"You're tearing our family apart, bro." Donavan walks toward the door. "Hope the pussy is worth it," he says as he leaves my office.

I need a drink.

TATE

How did I get myself roped into this? I agreed to meet up with Jenny, her friend, and her friend's mom at a mall to go dress shopping for a middle-school dance. I don't know a thing about taking girls shopping for dresses, but Jenny reached out to me, and I don't want to let her down.

I've only been seeing Decker a short time, but he and Jenny have become so important to me. I can't believe how protective I feel over them. I never knew I could care this much for two people so quickly. I'm falling in love with Decker. It's obvious even though I don't want to admit it to myself. He's all I ever think about.

The thought of confessing my feelings terrifies me more than shopping with teenage girls. I stare at myself in the mirror as I touch up my makeup in the company bathroom. Decker's going to drop me off at the mall and meet me afterward at my hotel.

I walk to my office, grab my clutch, and shut off the lights. Quinn is still at her desk. "You're here late."

Her cheeks redden. "Oh, umm, just getting things ready for Monday. Gotta think ahead and be prepared."

I observe one of Decker's twin brothers lingering in the doorway of his office but don't point it out. I never can tell them apart. I'm pretty sure she's got something going on with one of them. "What are your plans this weekend?"

"Me?"

I grin at her. "Who else would I be talking to?"

"Right. Umm, probably staying in." Her eyes dart around, then land back on mine.

"I'm having brunch tomorrow with some friends, you should come." If Decker and I become permanent, or serious at least, it would be nice to have more than one friend in this city.

"You want me to come to brunch with you?" Her brows knit. The situation borders on awkward.

"Only if you want to. No pressure. I'll text the address and you can come or not. I'm not the best at making girlfriends."

"Sounds fun. I'll be there."

"Good."

I spy Decker going to the elevator and rush off to join him.

As soon as the door closes, his mouth lands on mine

and I'm backed up against the wall. "Somebody's happy to see me." I grab the bulge in his pants.

"What can I say? I'm addicted." He wipes his mouth with the pad of his thumb, but only manages to smear my lipstick across his cheek. I laugh and debate on leaving it there, but considering we're still in his building, I give in and wipe it away with a wet wipe. I keep them in my clutch; with as many hands as I shake, I like to keep my fingers clean. One of my associates back in Dallas once made a comment about how every hand you shake could have been touching a dick or something like that, and ever since then, I've been more mindful of what I touch throughout the day.

Decker drops me off at Water Tower Place but not before groping me like a horny teenager in his car. If I wasn't meeting his daughter, I'd cancel my plans to get him into bed. I tease him but I'm just as infatuated with him as he is with me, if not more. I wake up every morning with a smile on my face thanks to him. I thought I had everything figured out, was content with my career and personal life but now that I've met him… I know I was settling. Coasting through. I don't want to coast anymore. I pull out my phone and fire off a text to Jenny.

Me - I'm here.

Jenny – Meet us in Free People. Third floor.

I find Jenny and her friend, Joselyn, and her mother, Patrice, in the dress section. Jenny's face lights up when she sees me. Her right hand lifts into an eager wave. I smile and wave back, making my way over. Her dark hair is swept up in a high ponytail, and she's dressed in skinny jeans and a graphic tee with strappy low-heeled sandals. Her friend has on a floral-patterned button-down shirt that looks like it belongs on the set of Little House on the Prairie.

I'm not one to be overly judgmental, but based on her friend's mother's style, it's no wonder Jenny called me in for backup. The poor woman dresses like she's going door to door selling bibles in an ankle-length denim skirt and oversized pink smock that does nothing to show her figure. They *all* need me; they need a style intervention. Jenny looks casual cute but still I still have the urge to raid her friend's closet and replace her wardrobe.

"Tate, this is Joselyn and her mom, Patrice. Guys this is my dad's girlfriend, Tate."

It's not lost on me that Jenny just called me her dad's girlfriend, and it's also not lost on me that I love the way she said it. It just rolled off her tongue, like it was a natural part of her vocabulary. "It's nice to meet you." I extend my hand to the mother.

"I've heard so much about you. It's nice to put a face with the name." She accepts my hand, but I feel her assessing me and wondering if I'm good enough for Decker and Jenny. It makes me happy to know she has Jenny's best interests in mind, and I'll show her my intentions with Jenny are pure and not just a means to impress her father. Jenny eyeballs a two-piece called the

Thalia. It's cotton-candy-pink with a crumpled top held up with two thin straps and a matching miniskirt that looks crinkled. It's adorable but I think Decker would kill me if we came home with anything that showed Jenny's midriff.

"What about this?" I finger through the rack and hold up a one-piece shoulder-wide legged pant set. It's a rust color that would pair beautifully with her skin tone, green eyes, and dark hair. And it doesn't show so much skin it'd give Decker a heart attack.

Jenny snatches the ensemble and rushes to the dressing room. I look her friend over as her mom holds up something red covered in flowers that would wash the poor girl out completely.

I grab an ivory dress with crochet panels that would be to die for with her dark hair and almond skin. "This would be so adorable on Joselyn." I hold it up and her mom gives me a wry smile.

She accepts the hanger and holds the dress up on her daughter. "I think you're right. You *are* good at this. I've never been very fashionable." As she runs a hand down her denim skirt, I think *oh, honey, don't I know it.*

She's a nice lady, but when it comes to style, I want to give her a good old southern *bless your heart.*

I smile at Patrice. "We could treat ourselves to something while we're here. I was gonna take the girls to get their nails done and thought we could get our toes done while they're doing that."

"Oh." She shakes her head. "I don't think..." She trails off and I can tell she never does things for herself.

"My treat."

"I couldn't."

"It'll be fun. The girls will enjoy it."

After trying two shoe stores, we find the perfect heels for both girls and make our way to the spa on the fourth floor to do a little pampering. Patrice seems to enjoy herself despite her reservations. Her olive eyes roll back in her head as her calves are being massaged.

My phone pings with a text from Decker.

Decker – How's it going?

Me – Checking up on me?

Decker – More like missing you.

Me – The girls want pizza but are afraid of messing up their manicures. I should have fed them first.

Decker – They'll live, but I won't. How much longer till I get you all to myself?

Me – Meet me in an hour.

Decker – Hey, Tate?

Me – Yeah?

Decker – Remember those bite marks?

Me – How could I forget?

Decker – There's going to be more of that.

He adds a little smiling devil emoji at the end of his last text. My heart races. This man is going to be the death of me.

TATE

Patrice drops me at the hotel, and I meet Decker in the lounge for a drink. I slide onto the barstool next to him and I already want to drag him up to my room. The man can rock a suit. That's for damn sure, and I'm used to seeing attractive men wearing suits. Decker puts them all to shame.

As I sidle up next to him, I say, "Come here often?"

He gives me a side eye. "Passing through on business." He plays along with me. "What are you drinking?"

"Something hard." I skim my fingers along his thigh.

"Should probably go easy. Plenty of time for hard stuff later." He shoots me a sly wink and orders me a bourbon drink with a hint of mint.

I take a sip. "Thanks for the drink. Care to join me for a nightcap?"

"I don't think my girlfriend would like that at all."

"I won't tell her." I make the motion of crossing my heart and sticking a needle in my eye.

He grins and slides his card to the bartender. "Can you keep a secret?"

I lean in close and whisper gently, my lips brushing against his earlobe. "What kind of secret keeper would I be if I told you?" I down my drink and grip him by the tie. "Let's go, lover." I move from the stool and sway my hips knowing he's appreciating the view of my ass.

Something about getting him worked up in advance sends heat racing between my thighs. The foreplay with Decker Collins is almost better than the sex.

Almost.

"Hate to kill the mood, but Donavan came by my office earlier."

"Yeah?"

"Wasn't happy about dropping the lawsuit."

I stop and turn to face him. "I don't want to come between you and your family."

"You're not."

I grin. "Yeah, I'm sure he spoke highly of me."

"Absolutely." Decker winks.

I shake my head. "I'm sorry. You don't need the extra stress."

Decker rakes a hand through his hair. "Agreed on that. I don't see any way around it, though."

We arrive in my room and Decker falls back on the couch while I excuse myself to the bathroom for a quick shower. I step under the spray of the water and lather up quickly, opting to wash my hair in the morning. It's our first night alone since we started seeing each other and I have plans for him. I'd planned on revealing my feelings, but after what happened between him and Donavan, I'm not sure it's the right time.

I massage lotion into my skin and put on the sexy underwear set I picked up at the mall while Jenny and her friend tried on dresses. It's a black lace corset and matching thong paired with thigh highs and a garter belt. Slipping on my black pointy toe heels, I stand at the mirror and run my fingers over my loose curls to smooth any strays. I feel sexy and powerful. Decker is getting a night he'll never forget. I step out of the bathroom ready to make my grand entrance only to find him snoring.

To say I'm disappointed would be an understatement, but I know he's been working so hard lately. He wants this merger over with so he can spend more time at home with Jenny, and I get the impression he may ask me to stay when the time comes. I've been trying not to think about that too much. I have so many things to consider. My job. My family. I'd be giving up a lot, but as I run my hand over Decker's head and along his jaw… I think he could be worth the risk.

He's so fiery and intense when he's awake, but when he sleeps, I can see a hint of the boy in him. It's that side of him I love the most. Him wearing his apron and cooking for Jenny or offering to run to the store for snacks while we watch Twilight.

I'm torn between letting him sleep or waking him up. Placing my lips to his and receiving no response, the choice is easy. He needs rest. Quietly, I strip out of my sexy getup and change into a tank top and comfy yoga-style leggings I normally reserve for the gym. I haven't been working out lately and it bothers me a little, but like Decker, I've been working crazy hours too. It's not lost on me that I've been getting in some quality cardio, though. I grab a pillow from the bed, prop his head up, and cover him with a blanket. Once he's taken care of, I turn out the lights and slide into the bed alone.

I'M NOT sure what time it is but I smile when I feel Decker's strong hands part my legs. The leggings I fell asleep in are already missing. His lips meet the sliver of skin between my panties and tank. I thread my fingers through his hair, yawn and simultaneously say, "Good morning."

A lazy grin crosses his face as he looks up to meet my sleepy-eyed gaze.

"Sorry I crashed out last night." He nuzzles my belly with his stubble-lined jaw.

"You were out cold. I started to wake you up, but you seemed so peaceful. You're getting old, Collins."

"Hah! Well, thanks for letting me sleep. I hadn't

realized how tired I was until my ass met the couch cushion."

"What time is it?" I can't see the clock but a quick glance at the window lets me know it's still dark out.

"Time for you to get naked and let me make last night up to you. I saw your little outfit in there and cursed myself for falling asleep. Sorry."

"If you're able to please me to my standards, I may model it for you sometime."

"Damn right you will." He kisses my stomach, pushing my top up to pay attention to my breasts. Sucking a nipple into his mouth, he appears to be done talking and focuses on getting down to business.

"Wanna get breakfast when we're done?"

Decker looks up at me like I'm insane for thinking about food while he has my breast in his mouth. "I plan on eating pussy for breakfast. More than one serving."

Only Decker Collins could turn me on with a breakfast metaphor involving my vagina. He quickly snaps me out of my thoughts when his tongue meets my clit. He's relentless and before long I'm squirming as he pulls an orgasm out of me with nothing but his tongue and fingers. My nails drag down his scalp as he raises up and stares at me while I pant for air.

A devilish grin spreads across his face, like he's admiring his handiwork and the way he knows how to press every one of my damn buttons to get me off.

"How'd I do? I think that was a record for time."

I shoot him the bird, but my limbs are so fatigued

from the intense orgasm my hand immediately drops back to the bed.

Decker laughs.

"It was a solid six. Not sure if it's worthy of a lingerie show."

He narrows his eyes at me. "Six my ass."

I shrug. "Looks like you may need some practice, champ."

"Oh yeah, do you say, '*Holy fuck, Decker. Right there. Jesus Christ,*' during all solid six performances?"

My cheeks flush and I look away, grinning. "Okay, maybe it was a seven."

He dives on top of me and tickles my ribs, and I can't think of the last time I let my hair down and had this much fun.

I ROLL out of bed looking at the time knowing I need to wash my hair and get ready to meet Alexis and her friends for brunch.

Decker lies there, naked, save for a sheet riding up his hip. He props himself up on an elbow in the Burt Reynolds pose, and it's difficult to look at him without wanting to jump back into bed. "Where you off to?"

"I have brunch plans with Alexis and some of her mommy friends."

Decker watches me dig through my clothes for something to wear. "You don't sound too enthused."

"I'm not."

"So why go? Come back to bed. Jenny won't be home until noon."

"Tempting, but I promised, and I invited Quinn. It'd be rude to bail and leave her on her own with complete strangers."

He gives me a perplexed look. "My assistant?"

I roll my eyes and grab my yellow heels. "*Our* assistant, and yes. She's nice, and I need a non-mommy ally. Someone who won't talk about boogers and puke."

Decker laughs and throws the sheets back exposing his thick erection.

"You can't be hard again?"

He wraps his fingers around his cock and strokes it. "What can I say? Watching you bend over fetching your shoes turned me on."

I try to ignore him, but he lays back on the bed looking like a damn Adonis in the flesh. His abs are like chiseled puzzle pieces and his jaw clenches with sheer determination. Why does he have to look so damn hot while jerking off? His teeth sink into his bottom lips as his mouth curls up in pleasure.

I war with myself for all of three seconds before I cross the room and straddle him. I line up his cock and ease myself down onto it.

His hand smacks my ass and he digs his fingers in. "That's what I thought."

"You're such an arrogant ass—"

He thrusts his hips up into me to cut off my sentence

and hits my spot just right. All my smartass remarks fade from my brain and are replaced with nothing but erogenous bliss.

"WHERE HAVE YOU BEEN?" Quinn hisses as I grab the chair next to hers on the rooftop at Cindy's. The restaurant and bar overlooks Millennium Park and Lake Michigan. Alexis grins at me, eyeballing the hickey on my collarbone. I wanted to nut-punch Decker for putting it on me this morning as I got ready. He did it right as I tried to get out of his car when he dropped me off. He's on his way home so he can be there in time for lunch with Jenny.

He attempted to get me to cancel on the girls and go home with him, but I couldn't do that to Quinn. Judging by the uneasy smile on her face it's a good thing I kept my word.

"Sorry. Got held up."

She eyes me with skepticism but doesn't press for information I don't want to share.

"We ordered already but I'm sure you still like pancakes," says Alexis, still seemingly amused at my love bite.

"I do. Thank you."

"So, Quinn says she works with you at the firm."

I nod and Alexis continues.

"I tried to pump her for information about your new boyfriend, but she wouldn't tell me anything."

My cheeks go red and I take a sip of the fruity drink they put in front of me. "Very funny. That's because there's nothing to tell. Aren't you going to introduce me to your friends?" I do my best to change the subject so I don't choke her out later.

She does nothing but sit there and grin. It's like we're in high school all over again, giving each other crap and playing practical jokes.

Alexis finally goes around the table and makes introductions. The other women look like Stepford wives and all they want to talk about are their husbands and children. It's like they have no other interest outside of their family life. I love spending time with Decker and Jenny but that will never be me.

I'm glad Quinn is here as a buffer. The two of us end up in our own conversation about the Collins brothers. "So, all of them are single?"

"Mhmm." She bobs her head.

"Do they ever date within the company?"

"No way, it's against policy. Well, it's against the rules for anyone considered a superior to date a subordinate, and they well, run the company."

"So, for example, if you were to enter into a relationship with Dexter… or say Deacon, you could be fired if it were reported?" I say each of their names slowly trying to gage her response but she's damn good at masking any tells. Usually, I can surmise if someone's lying or not in the first five seconds. It makes sense, though. She works in a law firm and deals with attorneys all day.

"How do you tell those two apart if they aren't in their office? I'm always confusing one for the other."

"Oh easy. Dexter has a scar over his brow and Deacon has a freckle on the pad of his thumb."

Bingo. I knew she was seeing one of them. How else would she know the man has a freckle on his thumb? I've never noticed anything distinguishable about the pair, but then again, my focus has been on Decker from day one.

We finally finish up and, on our way out, Quinn tells me to never make plans for us again. I laugh. She has a dry sense of humor. It's very subtle and you have to really pay attention to pick up on it. I like her a lot.

After parting ways with Quinn, Alexis gives me a ride back to my hotel. I thought about surprising Decker and showing up over there, but he really needs to spend some quality time with Jenny. I've been monopolizing his attention, and it's not very fair, considering how many hours he has to work until the merger is complete.

I need to work on a few things anyway, for when I go into the office on Monday.

TATE

THINGS HAVE BEEN GOING great between Decker and me. For the past three weeks I've spent my free time with him and Jenny, and I can't remember a three-week period in my life where I've been happier. I never stay in my hotel room anymore. Spending the night with him just feels natural.

I make sure to arrive at work separately even though I ride with him. The office doesn't need to know we're together, though I'm sure Quinn figured it out. Bless her for keeping it to herself. Decker needs to give her a raise for not gossiping like some of the women here who spread rumors in the cafeteria.

Quinn has been their target as of late. It hasn't gone unnoticed that an admirer sends her flowers every single Friday. I don't feed into watercooler gossip, but I keep my ears open for signs of trouble that could tank the merger. I trained myself to listen to the same rumor mills back in Dallas. Part of me feels guilty for spying on Decker and his employees but that's why I'm here. Regardless of my feelings, I have a job to do.

I walk down the hallway for my morning coffee while I get dressed. Decker cooks Jenny breakfast before school while she gets ready in her bedroom. She's complained all morning about what to wear. I remember being that age, feeling ugly in everything.

I have their morning routine down to a science at this point, and pretty much know everyone's daily schedule.

The doorbell rings and Jenny shouts from the stairs, "Uncle Weston!"

My face pales and I might vomit right there on the floor. I freeze and my stomach twists in a knot so hard it feels physically painful, even though I know it's all in my mind.

What the hell is he doing here?

I haven't told Weston anything about my personal involvement with Decker. I'd hoped we could avoid the conversation all together, at least until the merger goes through, but now… here we are.

Jenny tugs Weston around the corner and goes right past me. When his eyes meet mine, I want to dissolve into the hardwood floor. I don't think I've ever seen him this pissed off. I'm standing in Decker's freaking t-shirt and pajama pants. I've gotten used to wearing them when I stay over because they smell like him.

Weston glowers at me, but Jenny keeps moving him

toward the kitchen. I don't know what to do. Do I follow them and hope he doesn't make a big scene in front of Jenny?

I know he's irate. He's a ticking time bomb waiting to explode.

He speaks with Decker once he reaches the kitchen, and then he says, "If you'll excuse me, I need to step out and make a call."

"You don't want coffee?"

"Not right now."

Damn. I suck in a breath and hear his footsteps as he searches for me. It's like everything goes into slow motion and I'm in a horror film as the killer creeps through the house. Weston's footsteps grow louder with every second until they pound in my ears.

When he rounds the corner. His mouth forms a tight line and his jaw clenches. "Outside, now."

I nod, feeling like I might throw up. I've never screwed up at work, not once. Something tells me this might be unforgiveable. I knew he'd be upset, but I didn't think he'd be like this. He looks like he might fire me on the spot.

I walk with him out front, grabbing my wristlet as we go. I start to say something but he cuts me off.

"Not yet," he growls, grinding his teeth.

Knowing Weston and the way he keeps up appearances, he may shove me in a car and wait until we get to the hotel.

Instead, the second he's sure nobody can hear, he

wheels around on me. "What the fuck's going on here?" He whisper-screams his words and eyes my clothing like he's disgusted with what he sees. He raises a finger. "Hold that thought." He pulls out his phone and calls me a cab, the entire time holding his finger up to let me know not to utter a word. Once finished, he hangs up and says, "You have fifteen minutes. What the hell did I just walk in on?"

"It just happened, okay? But the merger is good to go. The BankIt suit was dropped. No other conflicts. Everything is ahead of schedule."

He sighs.

My temples throb. It's too damn early to have this conversation. I need coffee.

"Great. Since everything is squared away, get your ass back to Dallas. Don't pick up your things. I want you out of here *now*. I'll have my secretary make arrangements. Just show up at the gate. I'll have your stuff sent back."

"We're not finished. I still have matters to go over with Decker and his brothers. Nothing major. I need a few more weeks." I try to buy myself more time. I'm sure Weston sees right through it.

"No need. I'll find someone else. Someone who won't fuck the people we're doing business with."

Finally, the truth comes out.

"Why are you being an asshole about this?"

"Why am *I* being an asshole?" He shakes his head and shoves his hands in his pockets. "You're the smartest lawyer at the firm so I find it hard to believe you suddenly became blind as a fucking bat."

"Humor me."

"You kidding me with this shit? This deal is huge for our firm, and I won't see it fucked into a Chinese circus if you two have a falling out. Christ, look at you." His hand flies from his pocket and waves toward me.

I know I look rough. I'm dressed in Decker's clothes. My hair hasn't been brushed. We had a long night.

"I sent you here because you're the best I have. Who are you? What happened to my ball-busting shark?" He shakes his head like he doesn't even recognize me.

I swallow hard and try to push aside my feelings for Decker. I know some of what Weston says is true. I didn't come here to develop feelings for Decker. I look back at his front door with an uneasy sensation in my gut. "I can handle it." I shut my eyes tight and nod. "I can do this."

His features soften and he gives me a sad smile, almost like he pities me. "It's not personal so don't go full blown pussy on me. How much do I have to kiss your ass and tell you what a great attorney you are? You're my biggest asset. But you need to see this from a big picture perspective. Put yourself in my shoes."

I shift on my feet and keep my mouth closed. He's still my boss. I love my job. I don't argue. I can't, because he's right.

"If you were me, would you risk it? If I wanted to

date the partner of a firm you were merging with? With this type of money and all these jobs on the line? Think about all the employees and their families, and you're out here playing Russian Roulette with their livelihoods. Would you be cool with me doing the shit you're doing?" His voice raises up a notch.

I stare at the ground as he chastises me. The truth and weight of his words sink in hard. Decker and I were fooling ourselves.

"No." It guts me to agree with him, but I do. I let out a shaky breath and try to suck it up. This isn't like me.

"So, we're good?"

"We're good." I can't meet his eyes. I'm embarrassed. I'm hurt Decker knows I'm getting my ass chewed and isn't doing anything about it. I wouldn't expect him to change Weston's mind. I just figured he'd go to bat for me. I know Jenny's his main priority but what about me? What about us?

"Go wait for the cab. I'll deal with the rest. Once the merger is complete, I'll send you back. You can work it out. Decker's a great guy. I'm not trying to be a prick."

"I understand."

"Good. Call when you land."

I look back at Decker's front door and feel like I might shatter into a million pieces.

Weston pulls out his cell phone and calls his secretary to make flight arrangements.

I look down at my feet. I'm wearing flip flops, but it

doesn't matter. I'll buy something on the way. They have plenty of gift shops at the airport.

As I walk away, part of me hopes this will end like one of those scenes in the movies. Decker will rush out and tell me to stop. He'll tell me he doesn't want me to go, and he'll scoop me in his arms and carry me off to bed. But he doesn't. I reach the end of the driveway and look back one last time. Decker isn't coming and Weston has gone inside. The cab pulls up and all I can do is look at the house and try to lock it in my memory, in case I never make it back.

DECKER

JENNY RUSHES AROUND GRABBING her things, then scarfs down her breakfast.

Why did Weston drop in unannounced? He never stops by without putting something on the books.

I leave Jenny with Weston to check on Tate. I peek in my room and her clothes still hang on the back of my closet door. Her makeup bag is on the counter and the blow dryer is out. I walk through the house to see where she went. My jaw ticks when I come up empty.

Jenny calls out to me, "Dad, I'm leaving. Bus is here."

I meet her in the foyer and kiss her forehead. At the same time, I notice Tate's shoes by the door. "See you tonight. I'm making taco salad."

"Can't wait. Tell Tate I said bye."

I give her a nod. "Will do, slugger."

I wait until she gets on the bus. Once I know she's

headed to school, I return to the kitchen to confront Weston. It's no damn coincidence he showed up. Something's going on.

Weston seats himself at the counter and helps himself to coffee and a plate. He grins like an asshole and shovels food into his mouth. Taking his time, he dabs at his face with a napkin. His smile disappears when he sees the glare on my face. "For someone eager to get this merger completed you don't seem very happy to see me."

"Where's Tate? And what the hell are you doing here?"

Weston makes a show of pushing his plate away and standing up. He adjusts his suit and turns to face me. "Got a phone call. Didn't like what I heard. So, I decided to see how things were going. Didn't expect to find my senior attorney playing house with you and Jenny."

I move toward him, fists clenched at my sides. "Don't bring Jenny into this. That's a low fucking blow and you know it."

Weston shakes his head and smirks. "Someone needs to pull your head out of your ass. It's not personal."

"Yeah." I nod. "Business is business. So, you got a call?" *Fucking Donavan.*

He shakes his head like there's no way in hell he'll give up the source. "The phone call isn't important. You wanted this merger, remember? You came to me. Do I need to remind you what was said? Think about Jenny." He takes a second to collect himself. "Look, Tate's my best attorney. I can't afford her juggling all this right now."

I take another step toward him and grit my teeth. "Where is she?"

He scrubs a hand through his hair. "You need to relax."

"The hell I do. Where. Is. She?"

Weston lets out an exasperated breath and walks away, staring up at the ceiling. He finally turns back to face me and shakes his head like he can't believe he's dealing with any of this.

I can't really blame him. If I was in his shoes, I'd do the same thing. But, that's beside the point. This is Tate, and as much as Weston doesn't want it to be personal, it is.

Weston looks me dead in the eye. "You're not going to let this go, are you?"

I shake my head at him, telling him with my stare how determined I am and the lengths I'm willing to go.

"Fuck. I sent her to the airport, okay? I'll have someone else handle the last few things before we finalize our agreement. Once the merger is a done deal, I'll send her back if that's what the two of you want. It'll all work out. Trust me. I know what I'm doing."

I shake my head. It's not good enough. Not for me. Not for Tate. I already feel like I can't breathe without her and she hasn't left Chicago yet. "No."

"No?" Weston raises his eyebrows. He stares at me like I'm from outer space. "What do you mean no?"

I flatten my palms on the counter. "Tate stays or I terminate the merger." I look right at him when I say the words. She's that important to me. I'm willing to walk away from the deal of a lifetime. Jenny will understand. It'll break her heart if Tate leaves.

Weston lets out the most sarcastic laugh I've ever heard, like this all has to be a joke. "You can't be serious."

I step up so that our faces are inches apart. "Look at my eyes. Do I look like I'm joking?"

He stares at me.

I don't budge an inch. "I love her."

Weston scoffs, but I don't give a shit.

"Tate is everything to me. I didn't plan on this, but it happened. I *won't* lose her. Not for a second."

Weston's jaw clenches.

"Weston, you know I wouldn't let her around Jenny if it wasn't serious. How many women have you seen me bring home the last fourteen years?"

"None."

"Exactly. Jenny loves her too."

Weston paces back and forth. He pauses here and there, looks up at me, then glances away. He finally lets out an exasperated sigh and throws his hands up. "Fine. Fuck it. It's your life."

I damn near tackle him I hug him so hard. It wasn't planned, and it's a bit awkward. I finally lean back to maintain some dignity and put a hand on his shoulder. "Thank you. Seriously. You have no idea how much it means."

Weston brushes invisible dust off his shoulder where my hand was resting. "Well, what the hell are you waiting for? Go get the girl. I'm not fucking doing it for you. My generosity for the day has been concluded."

"She's on her way to O'Hare?" I'm damn near bouncing on the balls of my feet as I ask the question, and I'm positive my face is fixed in a permanent smile from ear-to-ear.

"She's probably almost there. Might want to throw your old cleats on and haul ass."

I slap him on the shoulder. "Thanks! I'll see you—fuck, I don't know when, but I'll see you."

"Don't come back without my all-star attorney. And stop acting like a pussy. I might vomit."

I snatch my keys off the hook and slip on the first pair of shoes I find on my way to the garage. I connect my phone to hands free and immediately call Tate, hoping I reach her before she gets on the damn plane.

I hammer the gas and my tires squeal as I get sent to voicemail. The car weaves through the morning traffic, and I curse anyone who gets in my way. "You want to fucking go?" I throw my hands up and bang on the horn.

I try her cell again with no luck. "Fuck." My face heats up to a thousand degrees. I smack the wheel as some asshole cuts me off. I'm going to fucking kill Donavan for calling Weston.

I shake my head to rid my thoughts of revenge and take a few deep breaths to calm down. Being angry will solve nothing. My goal is reaching Tate in time. Nothing else matters. The worst that can happen is she gets on the plane, then immediately gets on another plane back to me. I kick myself for not going to see what her and Weston were discussing in the front yard. If I'd had any idea he was sending her home, I'd have been out there in a heartbeat. I never imagined he'd ship her back to Dallas. She probably sat there wondering why I hadn't gone after her.

Fucking Weston.

It wasn't like that asshole didn't have the woman of his dreams already. I know for a fact one of his partners fell for his assistant, and she was a damn subordinate, not even an attorney.

One thing eats at my gut as my mind wanders to the worst possible places. What if Tate gets back to Dallas and decides Weston is right? What if she sees her family and realizes how much she'll miss them if she moves to Chicago? There are too many liabilities if she makes it back there. I have to have her, and I have to get to her before she gets on the plane. I wish I'd just told her how I felt before this morning. There's no way she'd leave if I'd just told her the truth.

I love her.

She's the one.

I hammer the gas even harder, and my car rockets down the highway.

TATE

I ARRIVE at the airport feeling like my life is falling apart. I know I screwed up my chance at being named a partner at the firm, but all I can think about is Decker. I'm hurt, embarrassed, lovesick… I reach for my phone and remember I left it on his nightstand. My heart squeezes at the thought of the man. I look down at my haggard appearance, feeling people staring at me—passing judgement. I look like a damn bum.

I make my way to a gift shop and purchase some leggings, a Welcome to Chicago t-shirt, and a pair of flats. It's not perfect, but it's passable for airplane attire.

I find the nearest bathroom to change. At least I have my wristlet with my ID and credit cards. I feel wretched and hope Jenny doesn't think I abandoned her. It sounds insane, but I love that kid to bits—her father too. I wish I'd told him how I felt. Maybe he'd have come after me in the driveway. Maybe he'd have talked some sense into Weston, pleaded with him for me to stay.

I know we haven't been serious for all that long, but I expected him to fight for me. The way he looks at me, the way he fucks me, the way he makes me feel and lets his guard down around me—I know he feels the same way I do about him.

I stop in the bathroom and splash cool water on my face, then dry it with paper towels. I look as rough as I feel. Like I've been run over by a damn semi. I need to slow down for a second, step back, and think things through.

How did my life go from amazing to pure shit in a matter of minutes? I should've gone by the hotel and packed my things, but Weston was insistent I come straight here. I wouldn't feel so lost if I had my stuff.

Why did he rush me out of there anyway? There must be a reason. A small part of me hopes he didn't tell Decker what he was doing. Maybe that's why he hurried me out of there, because he knew Decker would come after me. The probability of Decker chasing me down the driveway was high, but there's no way he'd leave and go to Dallas to find me. He wouldn't leave Jenny and his work at the office behind.

Fucking Weston. I swear that man always thinks three steps ahead when he plans something devious.

It's not like I can defy Weston and head back to Decker's house to see if that's what happened. He'd write me up for insubordination, possibly fire me if he was in a pissed off mood, which he is. And what if I'm wrong? Then I'd look like a complete idiot.

No, I have to get on this plane, head home, keep my nose down, and kick serious ass on whatever Weston assigns me. Once the merger is complete, I can come back. That's what I need to do, and pray Decker's feelings for me don't change in that timeframe.

It's going to be a long couple of months without seeing him and Jenny, but I have to suck it up and get things done.

I check in and receive my boarding pass. Weston wasn't messing around. I'm on the next flight to Dallas. One foot in front of the other, I head toward security. There's nothing I can do, and I feel helpless with each step.

My heart breaks a little more as I near security. A small part of me wishes I'd never come to Chicago. I thought I knew how a broken heart felt when I broke up with my first serious boyfriend at college. Looking back, it doesn't hold a candle this. It doesn't compare to the way my heart pinched in my chest and my stomach tied itself into a knot when Weston let me have it.

It's a shitty emotion—guilt. I'm not too familiar with it because I wall myself off from everyone except my family. Now, I begin to see why. My job is my life and I never fuck up at work, so I never experience the way my hands now tremble and the way every second now seems like an eternity.

Everywhere I look I see smiling faces, and I have

this unbelievable urge to scream at the top of my lungs. Right now, I just want one thing. I want to go home, chug a bottle of wine, and wallow in self-pity. I might even shed a few tears. Tomorrow, I'll be back to normal. That's what I tell myself anyway.

I arrive at security and get scanned. Since I don't have any bags, the process doesn't take long. I grab a magazine someone left when I arrive at my gate. I slink down into the seat and flip through the pages. Nothing holds my attention, but it gives me something to do.

A woman and her two kids take up the seats next to me. The baby is red-faced and screams at the top of his lungs.

My temples throb and my chest aches. There's a hole in my heart where Decker belongs. Across from me sits a couple who can't keep their hands off each other. They whisper sweet nothings and talk about the fun stuff they'll do on their honeymoon. My heart sinks further into my stomach. We weren't close to marriage, but I thought someday it could happen. It seems silly, but when you know, you just know.

I grab a coffee and hope the caffeine makes me feel better. More like myself. I'm not used to these emotions. I'm a hard ass. I'm Tate Reynolds. I don't do love and relationships. Maybe it *is* for the best I never told Decker the way I feel. The way I think about him constantly when he's not there. The way I might suffocate if he's not holding me. The way my heart comes alive when he looks in my direction.

"Now boarding flight 292 to Dallas." The loudspeaker interrupts my reverie.

Here goes nothing.

I grab my boarding pass and ID and head toward the gate. The line moves at snail speed.

It amplifies the crushing sensation of my heart being squeezed in a vise. For some reason, the closer I get to the tunnel, the more Decker fades from my life. I just want to get home and pretend none of this ever happened, but how do I let go of the cocky suit who turned my world upside down?

I move up in line behind the woman with the screaming baby and hope he doesn't cry the whole flight. I sound terrible, but my head can't take it. The worst headache of my life approaches at warp speed.

Then, I hear it. It's faint at first, and I barely make it out.

"Tate!"

It comes from far off in the distance, and I wonder if I'm imagining things.

Stop watching Sleepless in Seattle so much, Tate. Your life's not a romantic comedy.

It has to be in my head. I hand the gate attendant my boarding pass.

"Tate, wait!"

I freeze and grip the boarding pass so hard it creases in half. The attendant tries to take it, but I squeeze it harder. My body freezes, locked in time. It's not my imagination. I heard someone shout my name.

"TATE!" The voice booms and people stare and whisper.

I pull myself from a catatonic state and whip my head around.

My heart leaps in my chest, and pure happiness courses through my veins.

It's him.

He came after me.

Decker.

He sprints toward me—faster than I've ever seen any man run—nothing but focus and determination on his face. When he's about fifty feet away he smashes into another man. There's a tangle of limbs and suitcases. It doesn't stop him. He springs to his feet and continues toward me, not bothering to turn and offer an apology.

"Don't you dare get on that damn plane!" He screams the words, but he's panting, and they come out half jumbled.

He gets to the counter and snatches the ticket and shreds it up in front of us.

This can't be real. It's an out-of-body experience. I can't do anything but shake my head. "Wh-what are you doing here?" I know what he's doing here, but I want to hear him say it. I want him to work for it. And part of me knows this can't happen, no matter how bad I want him. Weston gave me strict orders and I can't lose my job.

"You're not going anywhere."

I reach out and grab his forearm. “Look, Decker, I appreciate you coming. It means the world to me, but we have to lay low for a few months until this is worked out. Weston will have my ass if I’m not on this plane.” I can’t fight back the emotions rushing through my body and I choke up as I say the words. A tear slides down my cheek. I quickly swipe it away hoping Decker doesn’t notice. I’m crying. I don’t cry. Not where anyone can see, anyway.

“You’re not going anywhere, *sweetheart*.”

“I have to go, Decker. Please. Don’t make this harder than it already is.”

He shakes his head and grips me by the shoulders. “You’re not listening. I talked to Weston. You’re staying.”

Before I can respond, Decker sweeps me up into his arms, bridal-style, forcing my arms around his neck.

For some reason, I can’t process what he says, but I’ll be damned if I ever let him put me down now that I’m in his arms. “What’d you do? Did you get me fired?” My brain isn’t firing on all cylinders. My head will explode if I don’t get the full story shortly.

Cheering people flank us on both sides. Decker growls his words as he carries me through the airport like a madman. “Stop thinking the worst for five minutes in your life. I wouldn’t do that to you.”

“What happened?”

“I told Weston, well…”

“Spit it out, Collins.”

He stops in the middle of the concourse and his eyes lock onto mine. It's the most serious I've ever seen him look. "I said if you didn't stay the merger was off."

The hackles on the back of my neck rise. "Are you fucking insane? He's going to kill me. Definitely fire me. And you won't be able to hire me if I stay, because he'll own the firm."

Decker laughs. The bastard laughs at me. I want to punch his face.

"You really think Weston is that big of an asshole?"

I raise my brows at him. Did he just ask that? "I thought you two were best friends for fuck's sake." Has he forgotten who we're talking about? Weston is a calculating, hard-nosed bastard when it comes to business.

Decker grins. "Fuck, he cracks the whip on you guys in Dallas, doesn't he?"

"Umm, yes, he does."

Decker plants a kiss on my forehead, then leans back. "Listen, Weston's a good guy. He might run a tight ship, but he's not heartless. He smiled when I left. Told me not to come back without you."

"You're bullshitting me."

"I wouldn't do that. Not about this. He knows I love you, Tate."

I gulp. "You love me?"

I glance around and notice a crowd around us, mostly women clutching their chests.

I stare at Decker for a few moments, our eyes

locked. His gaze is nothing but heat, intensity, and adoration. He's telling the truth.

"I should've told you before. I've loved you for a while, Tate Reynolds."

My heart might burst out of my chest. I had a feeling he did, but something about him saying the words sends a torrent of emotions crashing into me. Tears stream down my cheeks and I can't do anything but nod and nuzzle into his shoulder. "I love you too."

His arms tighten around me, then he pulls me up so we're face to face. He kisses me long and hard, with an urgency that says he'll never let go.

I pull back and grin. "Are you really carrying me like this through the airport?"

"Goddamn right I am, all the way to the car." Decker smirks.

God, I missed him so much, and I was only gone for an hour or two. It seems silly, like a teenage crush, but that's what it feels like. I think part of it was the thought I was leaving for good and had no idea if we'd ever be together again.

Not now, though. He's all mine, and I'm all his.

I curl up into his neck and enjoy the moment. "Just don't ever let go."

"Never, sweetheart." He kisses me once more, then carries me through the exit.

DECKER

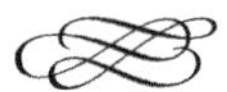

I GET Tate into my car and can't stop smiling. She has no clue how happy she makes me. From the moment I met her, I knew there was something about her, but I never dreamed she'd fit into my life so perfectly. She's what I've missed all these years. Now that I have her, I'll make every second count. I'm never letting her go again.

"Are we crazy?" She looks over at me. Her honey-brown eyes shimmer.

"Abso-fucking-lutely." I step on the gas. I can't get her home fast enough. I want her to move in. I know it's insane, but it feels right, and she needs a place to stay anyway. I don't want to scare her off, so I bottle the thought up for now, but I'll ask her soon. She can't live in a hotel forever and she's at my place most nights anyway.

She glances over to me. "How'd you get to me anyway?"

Her question takes me by surprise. "What?"

"How'd you get through security? They don't just let you waltz up to the gate."

"I bought a ticket."

Tate straightens up. "You what?"

"Well, if you left, I was going to have to follow you to Dallas."

The corners of her mouth curl up into a huge smile. She shakes her head at me.

"I have something on my face?"

"How could you come after me? You have Jenny and work."

"Didn't I tell you I'm in love with you back at the airport?"

"Yeah."

"There's something you need to know."

"What's that?"

"When I love someone, I go to the end of the earth for them. I already made plans for Molly to stay with Jenny, and I would've handled my management duties remotely. Nothing in this fucking world will keep me from you."

Tate leans over and gives me a peck on the cheek. Then, she slides around to my ear and whispers, "I love you too, Decker Collins." She pauses, and I feel her smile against my cheek. "And if it wasn't so dangerous, I'd suck your dick to show my appreciation." She flops back in her seat, clearly satisfied with herself.

"Fuck, woman." Her words leave me with a raging hard-on. I damn near pull over to the side of the road to remedy the situation.

I finally pull up my driveway and hope like hell Weston has left. I have plans for Tate. I'm going to make her scream my name on a loop. I exit the driver's side and move around to open her door.

"Such a gentleman." She grins her ass off, knowing what's in store.

We walk through the kitchen hand in hand. There's still a mess from breakfast this morning, but it can wait. Fucking Tate to the point of multiple orgasms can't. I want her in every way imaginable. I want her trembling beneath me.

I walk her toward the bedroom, removing her clothes along the way, leaving them behind like breadcrumbs.

Our lips connect. Her tongue flicks inside my mouth and dances with mine. I taste the coffee on her lips as I lick her mouth and neck.

I place my palms on her cheeks and our foreheads meet. "You'll never regret being with me."

"Ditto." Her breath fans over my lips.

Her hands cradle my neck as we do nothing but kiss. I lay her down on the bed. Her fingers tug on the hem of my shirt, lifting the white cotton over my head. I breathe Tate in. She smells like cinnamon and vanilla.

"God, I love you."

"I love you too, Decker."

I'll never get tired of hearing her say those words to me. Her breath hitches when I jerk her bra down and latch onto her nipple with my mouth. I take my time rolling the other between my fingers, teasing her. I repeat the motion, biting at her playfully, loving the sight of my gentle teeth marks engraved on her body.

Her slender fingers stroke through my hair. I see in her eyes how much she loves me as our bodies glide against one another. She skims her fingernails down my back, scratching lightly. She undoes my pants and shoves them down my legs with her feet until they tangle around my ankles.

I kick out of them and pepper kisses down her torso, rolling my tongue along the dip of her bellybutton. Another giggle escapes her lips and she twitches. I file away the ticklish spot for future torture. Gripping her panties, I jerk them to her feet and kiss her inner thigh, teasing her where she wants me most.

I smell her arousal and my cock grows harder. Looking at her folds, I can tell she's wet for me. I shimmy the black lace from her feet and toss it over my shoulder.

I roll over on my back, point to my face, and say, "Your pussy on my mouth, *now*."

There's no hesitation. Tate goes after what she wants, and I love that about her. Moving up the bed, she straddles my face in a reverse cowgirl position. I grip her hips and lower her inches from my mouth, then exhale my warm breath across her clit.

Goosebumps pebble over her ass and thighs and she shudders.

"You want to fuck my face, Tate?"

"God, Decker."

"Tell me you want my mouth on this pussy."

"Please," she moans.

I lick her slow, from clit to asshole, then pull my face back down away from her. She instinctively tries to shove her pussy against my lips, but I grip her ass and hold her away.

"Please, Decker? I'm so close." Her words trail away on a gasp.

That's what I like to hear. Her begging for my tongue. "Tell me who this pussy belongs to."

"It's yours, fu—"

I lick her again, just to interrupt her sentence.

She lets out a frustrated groan and says, "It's so yours. Trust me."

"Goddamn right it is." I shove her onto my mouth so hard it probably leaves a bruise.

She calls out my name as I lick, suck, and nibble.

Tate rocks forward, rolling her hips, riding my tongue and fingers, moaning the entire time.

Her hand wraps around my cock and she slides it up and down. Her tongue dances around my crown as she brushes a thumb over the head.

I groan against her pussy when she wraps her lips

around the tip of my dick. She bobs up and down, taking me as far in her throat as possible. The woman is the yin to my yang, her body molding perfectly to mine. We work together like a well-oiled machine. Before long, my cock pistons in and out of her mouth as I thrust up into her.

At the same time, I take two fingers deep in her pussy, pleasuring her g-spot as my tongue flicks over her clit. I don't need her to tell me she's close, I feel the energy radiating through her body.

Trembling over my mouth, she's about to lose it. I wrap my hands around her tiny waist and shove her against my face. My cock slides from her lips and she cries out. Every muscle in her body tenses at once. Her thighs threaten to crush my head as they squeeze together hard enough to crack a walnut. Her orgasm ripples through her body, coating my face with her wetness. I shove her down to the bed and slide out from beneath her. "Keep that fucking ass in the air and your face in the sheets."

Tate complies, gripping the sheets in her hands as she anticipates what's coming next. With one hand on her shoulder and one fisting my cock, I shove into her from behind. Her hot pussy cinches around me and nothing but pure ecstasy courses through my body. A moan tears from deep in her throat and she makes some pleas to the deity. Over and over again I slide in and out of her with deep punishing strokes.

Goddamn, I missed this.

Her ass claps against my thighs and the sounds reverberate through the room. Fuck, her pussy molds to my dick like it was created just for me. I'd planned on fucking her a lot longer, in every position imaginable, but now—watching her petite hourglass body rocking into me, the curls of her hair dancing across her back—I'm not sure how long I'll last.

Just when I think I can hold out a few seconds longer, her small hand reaches between her legs and she cradles my balls. The second she massages them and says, "That's it. Fuck your pussy, Decker," the orgasm I'd been holding rushes up my shaft.

"Fuck, Tate…" My words trail off and my whole body stiffens. I hold back as long as I can, then grab both her hips and yank her as hard as I can back into me.

I want to be buried as deep inside Tate as humanly possible, joined together as one when I explode inside her. Her frantic hands paw at the sheets and I look down as she bites into a pillow.

I groan and let loose, pumping into her sweet cunt. After a few grunts, her pussy contracts around me and she milks the last bit of come from my cock.

I slide out of her and she crawls up next to me as I pull her into a tight embrace, kissing her on the temple. I push a few sweaty strands of hair from her cheek. "Glad I caught you in time."

"Me too." Her arms squeeze tight around my middle, her head resting on my chest. She nuzzles into me and I could seriously lie here like this for the rest of my life.

Words can't adequately describe the pure joy taking over my body right now. It's better than any drug in the world, that's for damn sure.

"Move in with me. With Jenny and me." I don't ask. I tell her.

Pulling away, she looks up at me and smiles big. "Promise you'll never let me go?"

"Never, babe. Never." I bring my mouth down on hers, sealing my promise with a kiss.

DECKER

"IT'S SO HOT." Jenny fans a hand in front of her face as we walk to the rental car. I'd laugh but I'm sweating too. Neither of us are used to this heat.

"That's Texas for you."

"Dad, I'm seriously melting."

I unlock the jeep I rented for the weekend and stick our bags in the backseat. It's been a little over three months since the airport rescue, as I like to call it. Tate's been here in Dallas the past two weeks organizing her move to Chicago. I wanted to come down sooner but couldn't get away from the firm.

My phone rings. Speaking of the woman who owns my heart. "Hey."

"When can I see you?"

"Soon. I'm just getting in the rental. I'll be at the hotel within the hour if traffic isn't a nightmare." I didn't tell her Jenny's with me. She was supposed to stay with Joselyn, but they had a fight over a boy, and I decided to bring her along.

"Drive safe. I love you."

"Love you too, sweetheart."

I end the call and tuck the phone back in my pocket. Jenny buckles in on the passenger side and groans for me to get the air conditioning rolling. "Let's go, Dad. I'm dying." She twists the cap off a water bottle and chugs.

I climb into the driver's side, eager to see Tate. Sure, we've video chatted every night but it's not the same.

After fighting traffic for forty-five minutes we arrive at the hotel. We check in and take our bags up to the room. Tate's supposed to meet me here before dinner at her brother's house. She's dying to show me off. Her words not mine. I'm a little nervous. This is a huge step. Being introduced to family makes it all real.

Jenny goes into the bathroom to change and when she comes out, I nearly have a heart attack. My baby girl looks like a woman in a cotton-candy-pink miniskirt and matching top that has the thinnest straps I've ever seen.

"Do you like it?" She twirls around.

"What the hell are you wearing?"

"Dad!" Jenny glares at me.

I never really curse in front of her, even though I don't think hell is actually a curse word. It was probably the way I said it.

"What? Okay, sorry, go back in and come out and try again."

She throws up her hands and huffs her frustration, then goes in the bathroom and walks back out. She plasters the fakest, most sarcastic smile on her face and says, "Do you like it?"

I never really thought Jenny was much like me. She's always so sweet and innocent, but as her teen years continue, I see more of myself in her every day.

I think carefully about what I say next. Fucking women, they cause you to overanalyze everything. "It's umm, you look beautiful in it. Maybe a little, umm, too beautiful, though?"

She shakes her head at me like she wants to say *really*?

I'm sure I fucked up somehow and she'll let me know about it for days.

She twirls around and reveals she's wearing shorts underneath.

Thank fuck, but still… if this is how she plans on dressing I'm going to end up in an early grave or send somebody to one for looking at her. It's too mature.

She grins her ass off and raises her eyebrows. "Tate bought it for me."

My jaw clenches. *Goddamn it, Tate.* I'm going to take her over my knee and spank her ass when I get my hands on her.

There's a knock on the door and I open it. It's Tate. She leaps into my arms. Her legs wrap around my waist and her mouth crashes into mine. She grinds against my cock and I'm met with a raging hard-on coupled with embarrassment.

I pull back and lick my lips, sliding her down to the floor. Maybe it wasn't the greatest idea not telling her Jenny was coming.

Her face goes red when she sees Jenny behind me. "Oh. Hey, sweetie. I had no idea you were coming this weekend." She says the last sentence through gritted teeth as she turns her head to look right into my eyes. She plasters on a fake smile, then turns back to Jenny. "And you look adorable."

Thank God I have the outfit she bought as leverage. "So this was your idea?" I wave a hand in front of my daughter.

"Err… well I thought it was cute and she loved it when we were shopping for her dance."

The vein in my neck starts to pulse. "Jenny, go change."

"But, Dad."

"Now please." I narrow my eyes on Tate.

Jenny stomps back into the bathroom on the verge of tears.

Tate folds her arms and looks up at the ceiling.

"You're in big trouble, *sweetheart*." I step into her space and move her arms away from her body. My mouth goes to her neck and I bite down in a playful way.

"It was a gift." Her tone is soft.

"I know, and she can wear it as a bathing suit cover-up to the pool." I scrub a hand over my face. "I swear to God, are you trying to give me a heart attack? I'm going to spank your ass for this."

"Is that a warning?" She smirks.

"It's a promise."

"I'll tell you what. Let Jenny wear her new outfit, and I'll take the spankings for it."

I lean back and grin my ass off. "It seems like you both win in that scenario."

"I should've never picked a smart one." Tate slides a hand up my chest, obviously trying to butter me up so Jenny can wear her new outfit.

I'm no fool. I know exactly what she's doing, but it still always seems to work somehow.

"I'll never tell you how to parent, Decker. But I am a woman, which means I was a teenage girl once. If you try to force Jenny into doing whatever you want, well…" She whistles as her words trail off. "You're gonna have a rough time, bucko."

"I don't want my daughter dressing like…"

"A slut?"

I point a finger at her, not in a menacing way. "I didn't say that."

"You say it to me in the bedroom all the time." She waggles her eyebrows, clearly enjoying fucking with me.

Goddamn women!

"That's exactly why she shouldn't be wearing that shit."

"Decker, Decker, Decker. Think through this problem like an attorney and not an emotional father. Let's look at the facts, okay?"

I shrug. "Okay." She'll tell me anyway, whether I want her to or not. But she does have a point. I want my relationship with Jenny to stay strong, even though I know she's growing up and becoming more independent.

"Your daughter is the sweetest child. She's smart, funny, adorable, incredibly mature for her age, and she makes fantastic decisions. You trust her, right?"

"Of course I do. I trust her more than I trust me to make good decisions."

"What's it going to hurt for her to wear that outfit while she's down here? Did you feel the heat outside? It's not like she's wearing it to a club or party or down a dark alley late at night."

I hold up a hand because I'm already tired of the conversation, and I don't need her to tell me how wrong I am any longer. "Jenny?" I holler out the side of my mouth.

Jenny walks out in the clothes she wore on the way over. "Yeah?" She does not sound enthusiastic as she asks the question.

"You can wear the outfit here."

Her eyes light up. "I can?"

"Yes, it was a gift. But don't make a habit of this, okay?"

She rushes over and grips me in a bear hug. "Thank you so much, Dad!"

"You're welcome, slugger." I plant a kiss on her forehead.

She turns to Tate. "You talked him into it, didn't you?"

Tate glances up at me with an evil grin, like she's about to betray me. We both know she is. "Of course I did, sweetie."

"So, it's really you I should be thanking." They both grin at me, knowing how much they love to get under my skin and see me all riled up.

I just throw my hands up. "Can we get on with our day please? You two are killing me."

"Awww." Tate grabs one of my cheeks and they both wrap their arms around me and hug at the same time. "We love you, Decker."

"Yeah, Dad. You know we love you."

As frustrated as they might make me sometimes, I wouldn't trade these two for anything in the world. This is my life. My family.

EPILOGUE

TATE

Six months later

"You almost ready, babe?" Decker calls to me from the bedroom.

"Just finishing my hair." I look over my reflection and that one curl that always gives me trouble is actually behaving tonight.

Decker walks up behind me. His hands land on my hips and his mouth at my ear. "Fuck, you're beautiful."

"Not looking so bad yourself."

He kisses my neck. "Think anyone will miss us if we show up late?"

"They'd definitely miss *you.* You worked your ass off to make this merger a reality and now it's finally paying dividends."

"Oh, they'd miss you too. How did I get so lucky to secure you in the deal?" He grins at me in the mirror.

"Secure me?" I scoff, twisting around to face him. I put a palm to his chest.

"Damn right. Your ass belongs to me in perpetuity." He knows when he drops his voice down low like that, I can't resist him. It makes me weak in the knees.

"I think you better take me to this party." I wink and start toward the car.

Decker follows me out, dressed in his best suit. My favorite one. It's a dark blue Hugo Boss with a light blue shirt that makes his eyes pop. I'm a lucky woman. We've been living together for the past three months. It took some convincing to get me to agree. I didn't want to jump in too fast although I stayed over nearly every night anyway.

We make it to the firm's cafeteria, and it has been transformed. Everything is so fancy with catered food, linen-covered tables, twinkling lights, champagne, ice sculptures. We enter and Decker is well received. People pull him in ten different directions, but he keeps a tight hold on my hand. The main players from The Hunter Group are all present. Weston is here with his wife, Brooke. She runs a nonprofit for women and children. Brodie has April on his arm; she designed the dress I'm wearing. Jaxson is with his longtime love, Jenna. Maxwell shows off Claire, and I smile to myself. She's wearing a new collar. They're freaks in the sheets, that's for damn sure. The stuff she tells me would make a porn star blush.

Weston and Decker shake hands. Jaxson steals Decker for a minute and Weston leans in and whispers, "You two make a nice couple. Glad you didn't fuck it up."

I shake my head and smile. "Yeah, glad *I* didn't fuck it up. That's a good one, boss."

Weston moves off to mingle, leaving me alone with the rest of the Collins brothers. Some of my female coworkers from Dallas strut past us.

"Maybe this shit show will work out after all..." Donavan trails off, smirking, his gaze following them across the room.

He and Decker have been at war over everything the last six months. I think Decker is more hurt than pissed off, to be honest.

I smile at the brothers. "Told you, boys. The women are better in Texas, and smarter too, so you probably don't stand a chance."

Deacon laughs. "We'll see about that. This ain't golf, darlin'," he says, practicing his southern drawl.

"Yeah, you can't find the hole under any circumstances."

Dexter dies laughing, while Deacon pretends he needs someone to administer CPR.

As they walk off toward the bar, Dexter says to Deacon, "She's the fucking queen of burns. I don't know why you do that to yourself."

I can't help but grin. Decker's brothers—at least the twins—are slowly becoming more tolerable.

I sip on my cocktail and watch the party in motion around me, proud of the work Decker has done.

Decker comes up from behind and wraps his arms around me, interlacing his fingers across my stomach. "Still hate my brothers?"

"They're growing on me."

"Something's growing on me too." His voice is low and seductive in my ear.

"We're at a work party." I spin and smack at his chest.

He puts a palm over my hand and gives me that smoldering stare that sends my heart racing. "Come with me."

I follow, unable to say no.

He escorts me out to the roof deck. The city is lit up with Lake Michigan in the backdrop. Lights reflect off the rippling water. It's beautiful up here at night. Like a scene out of a movie.

"Sweetheart." He takes both my hands in his. "The day we met, I knew there was something special about you. I never imagined what would follow. I never imagined I'd find someone who could fit into mine and Jenny's lives so seamlessly. You put me in my place more times than I can count. You put up with me. You know me better than anyone. You're my best friend. My partner. The only woman…" He pauses and drops to one knee.

Tears stream from my eyes, and I both hate and love that he can turn me into a blubbering mess.

Once down on his knee, Decker continues, "I want to share my life with. Will you marry me?"

He drops my hand and produces a giant diamond solitaire from his pocket.

My hand shoots up over my mouth as I nod through my tears. "Yes. Yes, I'll marry you." I bolt into him, nearly knocking him off balance, but he catches me. He hooks an arm around my waist.

Our mouths collide and I can't stop crying long enough to fully kiss him back.

After a long embrace, Decker pulls back and slips the princess-cut diamond ring on my finger. I can't stop staring at it sparkling in the moonlight.

He looks over my shoulder and says, "Did you get it? Please tell me you got it."

Jenny pops out from behind one of the deck chairs with her phone. She sniffles and has to wipe tears from her eyes as she nods. "Yeah, Dad, I got it all."

"Where did you come from?"

"Uncle Weston snuck me up here." She turns to her father and puts a hand on his chest. "Oh. My. God. Dad, you were amazing. You did it even better than when we practiced."

I turn to Decker. "You practiced this? With Jenny?"

Decker shrugs. "Wanted it to be perfect."

Decker starts to say something, but Jenny squeals and practically tackles me. "I'm so happy for you two."

"Thanks. And thanks for showing your dad how to do that. I'm sure you wrote the speech for him."

Jenny turns to her father and beams with pride. "Actually, he was adamant that I didn't help him with it. He wanted it to come from the heart."

She holds up my hand like it's a display and inspects the ring. "Look how beautiful it looks on her hand, Dad."

Decker nods and they both stare at it.

After a few quick seconds, Decker brings us both in for a hug. "My two ladies. I love you both so much."

Jenny and I in unison say, "We love you too."

The party seems like an afterthought now. I just want to stand here with my two favorite people in Chicago and stare out at Lake Michigan forever. I know without a doubt this is it… this is my happily ever after.

POSSESSIVE PLAYBOY PREVIEW

When I first took a job at a law firm, I never thought I'd end up in a supply closet with a partner balls-deep inside me.

Oh, and it's not just any partner seconds away from curling my toes—it's Deacon Collins. My boss's brother.

The shameful part is it's not the first time.

Not even close.

I need to put a stop to it. These quickies are becoming more and more frequent, and I tell myself it's the last after each one.

"Fuck, Quinn." His tone is raspy as his lips drag down the side of my neck. He's possessive and hungry, nipping his teeth along my collarbone as he thrusts into me from behind.

A large, firm hand slides up my thigh, and yanks my white panties farther across my ass. I wore them for him. There's something about white seeming virginal that turns him on. I shouldn't encourage his fantasies, but I do. We're playing a dangerous game, sneaking around in a place where we could easily be caught. I think that's part of the thrill for both of us.

I inhale a breath, taking in his masculine scent. There's something primal and raw about Deacon Collins.

He slides out of me and I immediately miss the connection.

My skirt rides farther up my ass as he lifts me onto the counter. I wrap my legs around his waist and smirk over his shoulder when I spot new storage containers in the corner. They're filled with everything that once occupied the space where I'm sitting. "Clean up for me?"

"Shit was always in my way." His hazelnut breath fans over my lips as he leans in closer to kiss me.

He gazes at me with gray eyes that remind me of a storm approaching. His torturous fingers rub over my clit and I don't know how much more I can take. Deacon loves to toy with me—tease me. He always needs to be in complete control.

His favorite thing to do is bring me to the edge of release then yank me back over and over.

"Gonna come for me, my dirty little office slut?"

I roll my eyes at him, pretending to be annoyed, but my body betrays me, trembling under his touch. Truth is I would kick his smirking ass if he said anything like that to me anywhere else. But when he's buried inside me, there's something about it that drives me insane.

"Less talking, please."

"Keep mouthing off and I won't let you come at all."

"I can get myself off."

Deacon shakes his head and slides a hand up until it's wrapped around my throat.

My eyes widen.

Deacon smirks. "Not like I can."

I can't argue with him, because he's telling the truth.

Right when I start to mouth something back at him, he shoves in deep and hits my spot just right. I have no earthly clue how this man knows how to push my buttons the way he does.

My walls squeeze around him, craving more. I squirm on the counter, a slave to his touch.

Grabbing a fistful of my hair with his free hand, he growls his words. "Not running that mouth, now. Are you?"

"You like my mouth when your dick's in it."

His eyes roll back for a second, then land on mine. "Fuck, woman."

"That's what you need to do, because we're almost out of time."

The cocky bastard slips out of me, yanks my panties down, drops to his knees, and pushes my legs farther apart. I know he does it just because I told him to fuck me harder in a roundabout way.

Deacon moves in, flicking his wicked tongue across my clit. "I'll fuck you when I'm damn good and ready."

I rake my nails through his hair. His confidence is off the charts hot, but he needs to take care of business. People will come looking for us soon.

Finally, after teasing me for what seems like an eternity, Deacon lines up with my entrance.

My fingernails bite into his sculpted ass as he slides the head over my clit.

"This what you want?" He grins down at me and eases in.

My head rolls back. When I'm with Deacon all my worries seem to fade away. Maybe it's why I continue to do this—have sex with him in random places around the office. He gives me an escape I can't get anywhere else. Believe me, I've tried.

I've never been this girl. The girl who wears tight skirts because she knows it turns a man on, but I morph into a different person around him.

His thighs smack into my ass. "If you're staring off in space, I'm not fucking you right."

"No, you're perfect. Don't stop." I gasp when he draws out and slams back in harder.

Gripping my hips, Deacon increases the tempo until my mind is nothing but a blur. Thrusting in and out harder and faster, the man has his own agenda now, and I happily race him to the finish line. My head bounces off the cabinet behind me, but I don't care. I ride the wave of pleasure coursing through my body.

His stormy eyes sear into me. His stare feels way too intimate for our relationship. Well, our hooking up. I wouldn't call what we have a relationship. I like his dick and he's willing to use it on my terms. No strings attached. We both get what we want—the satisfaction of getting off.

I clench around him and a spasm hits me. Deacon's lips find mine and he grunts against them as he comes. We both jolt a few more times—he groans, I moan his name.

Eventually, we're both reduced to nothing but rough pants and smiles.

"Fuck, that was fantastic."

I put a hand on each of his shoulders and push him off me. "Fun's over."

Stepping back, he removes the condom, shoves it in his pocket, and pulls his pants up.

"Gross, Deacon, you're going to ruin your suit." My nose wrinkles.

"Should I carry it out of here in my fingertips?" He shakes his head at me, laughing.

Fair point.

I hop off the counter and pull my skirt down then hold my hand out. "Panties?"

He waggles his eyebrows. "Finders keepers."

I roll my eyes and smooth my hands over my hair. I don't know what his obsession is with my underwear.

"Let's grab dinner tonight."

I freeze. What did he just say? "Like a date?" I snicker. "You *must* be joking."

"Why's that funny?" His brows draw inward as if my words have wounded him.

What the hell?

"Come on, Deacon. We know what this is."

"What's wrong with going on a date with me?"

I exhale a sigh. "Where should I start? You're a player. We both agreed this was casual. Please don't get weird about this. It's fine the way it is."

"Can't two friends share a meal?"

"We're not friends."

Take the hint, sir!

He shrugs. "Colleagues share meals."

"Enough, Deacon." I need this conversation to end. "It's against company policy. You have a meeting to get to."

Deacon takes one of my hands in his and he looks more determined than I've ever seen him. "I'm not giving up on this. It *will* happen."

I shake my head. He'll grow tired of me soon enough and move on to the next girl. It's what he does.

He stuffs his shirt back into his pants and adjusts his Hugo Boss jacket.

Reaching out, his fingers stroke my cheek. "You're flushed."

I suck in a deep breath and fight the urge to lean into his hand. There's just something that feels natural about it, but I know better. The man is anything but an adult.

There's no way he could handle an actual relationship. He takes nothing seriously. I'm not foolish enough to believe I could be the exception.

With a parting smile he slips through the door quietly, taking what seems like all the air with him.

I inhale a few deep breaths to calm myself. There's too much at stake for me to catch feelings for Deacon Collins. I grab a few pens, Wite-Out, and a pad of legal paper so it looks like I have a legitimate reason for being in here.

My eyes flick back and forth as I walk out. Nobody is around, thank God. The last thing I need is to become the hot gossip item at the office.

I place stuff from the closet in the bottom drawer of my desk. Deacon exits the bathroom and struts past me wearing a smile so big it might get stuck to his smug face.

"Back to work, slacker."

I scowl at him. *Jerk.*

When he reaches his office, I promise myself I won't give him the satisfaction of catching me staring his direction.

The heat of his gaze burns into my head, though. I lift my eyes, ever so subtly in his direction, and the bastard winks right at me.

Damn it!

I really need to end this.

Possessive Playboy coming November 1st!

ACKNOWLEDGMENTS

First, we'd like to thank our families, Mrs. H and the Boy, and Chelle Bliss. Without their patience and understanding, this book would never have happened.

Lauren L-something Whateverson, thank you so much for all your hard work and for putting up with the two of us. You're a saint.

Jean Siska, we can't thank you enough for your legal expertise. You make sure we don't sound like fools who know nothing about attorneys, and we're grateful for that. You're a rockstar!

Trina and Stacey at Underline This Editing. Thanks for making sure our manuscripts are typo free and ready for readers. You're the best!

Our groups, the Harem and the Den, thank all of you amazing ladies (and a few men) who read, share, post awesome gifs, and generally keep us psyched 24/7 about what we're working on. Your support means the world to us and we couldn't do this without you.

To anyone we missed, sorry! It wasn't intentional, but we do thank you!

ALSO BY SLOANE HOWELL

GET A FREE BOOK BY SIGNING UP FOR MY NEWSLETTER

One of my favorite things about writing is building a relationship with readers. Join my newsletter for information on new books and exclusive deals plus a free copy of Panty Whisperer: Volume 1.

You can get this book for **FREE** by signing up! **(click here)**

You can read more Sloane Howell books by clicking on the book below.

Bossed

Scored

The Matriarch

Panty Whisperer

Bad Dad

Savage Beast

NOVELLAS:

Tommy Boy

Alpha Bad Boys

Chloe Comes for Christmas

Also by Alex Wolf

Want to read more about Weston and the Hunter Group?
Tap on the picture above!

COCKY SUITS BOXSET

Damon

Naughty Girl

Rock God

Guitar God

A Bad Boy for Christmas

Shagged

Professor's Pet

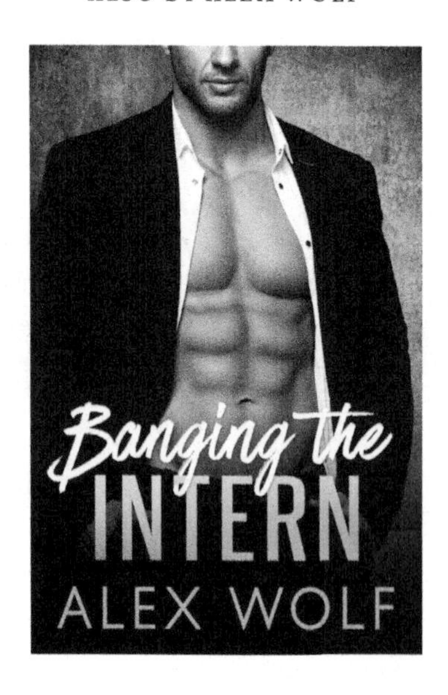

You can get your FREE ebook of Banging the Intern by tapping HERE!

ABOUT ALEX WOLF

Alex hails from the Midwest and currently resides in Tampa, Florida with his girlfriend Chelle, his son and two cats. His daughter is currently serving in the U.S. Navy. He's a huge fan of THE Ohio State Buckeyes and the Cleveland Browns.

O-H…

He enjoys writing steamy romance but more importantly he enjoys the "research" required to produce the steamy scenes. If you like filthy-mouthed, possessive alpha heroes and steamy romance, then he's the author for you!

Join my PRIVATE facebook group!
Join Alex Wolf's Den

Sign up for my newsletter and be the first to know about future releases!
Sign me up!

Where you can follow me